Ms. Rapscott's Girls

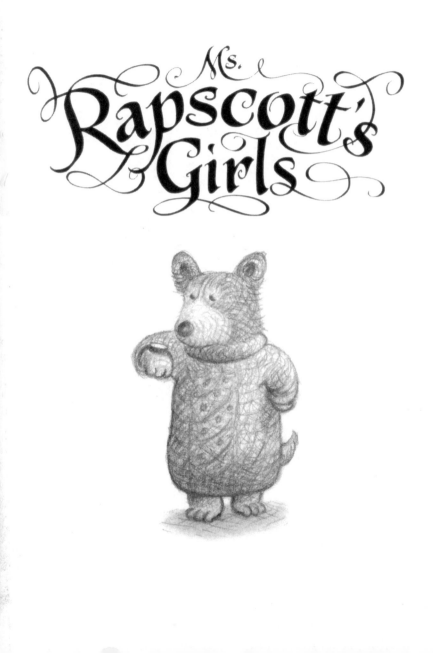

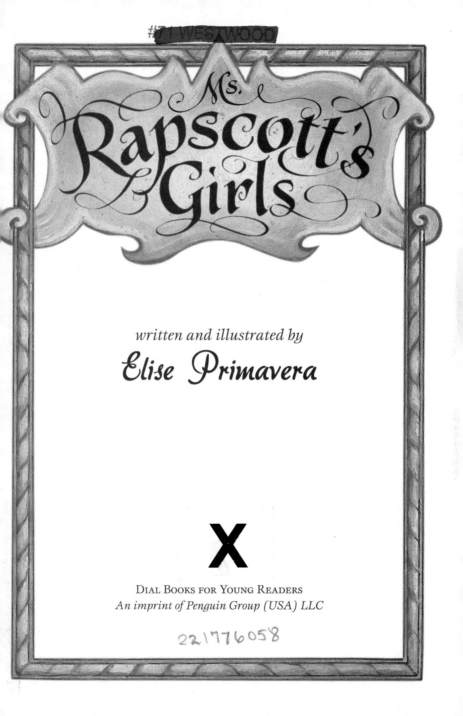

Ms. Rapscott's Girls

written and illustrated by

Elise Primavera

X

DIAL BOOKS FOR YOUNG READERS
An imprint of Penguin Group (USA) LLC

DIAL BOOKS FOR YOUNG READERS
Published by the Penguin Group
Penguin Group (USA) LLC
375 Hudson Street
New York, New York 10014

USA / Canada / UK / Ireland / Australia / New Zealand / India / South Africa / China
PENGUIN.COM
A Penguin Random House Company

Library of Congress Cataloging-in-Publication Data
Primavera, Elise.
Ms. Rapscott's girls / by Elise Primavera.
    pages cm
Summary: "At Great Rapscott School for Girls of Busy Parents, Ms. Rapscott teaches her students
How to Get Lost on Purpose, resulting in a series of fantastical adventures that make each learn a
little something about courage, strength, bravery, and teamwork"— Provided by publisher.
    ISBN 978-0-8037-3822-5 (hardcover)
[1. Teachers—Fiction. 2. Eccentrics and eccentricities—Fiction. 3. Adventure and adventurers—
Fiction. 4. Life skills—Fiction. 5. Conduct of life—Fiction. 6. Boarding schools—Fiction.
7. Schools—Fiction.] I. Title.
PZ7.P9354Ms 2015
[Fic]—dc23   2013032928

Manufactured in the United States on acid-free paper
10 9 8 7 6 5 4 3 2 1

Designed by Jennifer Kelly
Calligraphy by Judythe Sieck
Text set in ITC Esprit Std

For Lily Baye and Madden Rose,
who will *never* be mailed to Ms. Rapscott

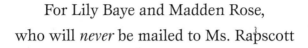

GREAT

RAPSCOTT

SCHOOL for GIRLS of BUSY PARENTS

ATTENTION, BUSY PARENTS!

Great Rapscott School for Girls of Busy Parents
has a unique curriculum designed solely
for your daughter.

Including our essential introductory program:

How to Find Your Way

Plus! **everything** your daughter needs to
know that you are too busy to teach her!

We understand that you are too busy to even
apply for admission for your daughter, so we
will be sending a letter of acceptance shortly! *

Too busy to bring your daughter to
Great Rapscott School?
Not a Problem!
For your convenience we have provided this
easy to use self-addressed box in which to
safely mail your precious daughter.

No postage necessary. Crackers and cheese are free.

_____

* Great Rapscott School is exclusive *only* to the daughters
of the busiest parents **in the entire world**.

OUR MOTTO: "Adventure is worthwhile in itself!"
—Amelia Earhart

Dear Dr. Loulou Chissel & Dr. Lou Chissel,

It has come to our attention that you are one of the *five* busiest parents **in the entire world.** And so...
We are happy to inform you that **Beatrice** has been selected for admission.

Congratulations!

Sincerely,

Ms. Rapscott

Ms. Rapscott
DIRECTOR OF ADMISSIONS
GREAT RAPSCOTT SCHOOL FOR GIRLS OF BUSY PARENTS
BIG WHITE LIGHTHOUSE BY THE SEA

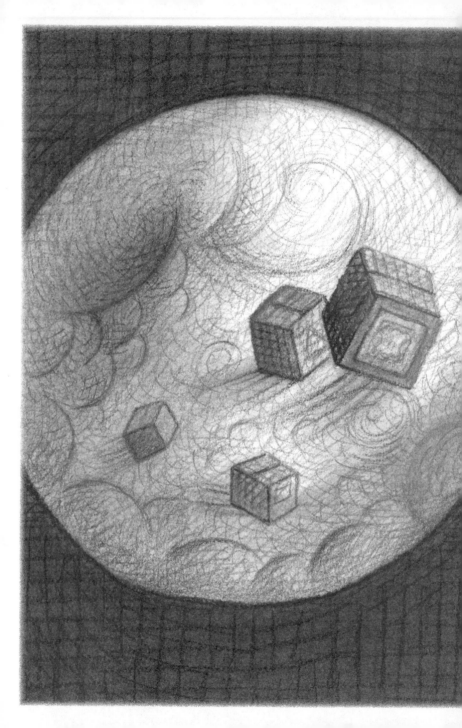

Chapter 1
ℬEATRICE

It was a perfect day for getting Lost on Purpose.

Ms. Rapscott stood at dawn on the observation deck of the lighthouse that was Great Rapscott School for Girls of Busy Parents. A huge beam of light rotated slowly above her. The teacher peered through binoculars while her two corgis looked on.

Armies of dark clouds marched ominously in from the west. The weather would be bad—but here in Big White Lighthouse by the Sea the weather was always bad. "Do you think it will storm, boys?"

Lewis licked the tip of a paw and held it up in the air to check the direction of the wind. Clark nodded a confirmation; it *would* most likely storm.

Ms. Rapscott scanned the horizon and, in the distance, she saw five faint objects whizzing through the air. They were in a V formation—a pattern used by geese flying south for the winter. But these were not geese, these were boxes—five large boxes. They flew north over the sea road that snaked along the cliff of the rocky coast, straight for the school. "They're here!" She hurried inside, and clattered around and around, down the circular staircase. Lewis remembered his watch and hurried to strap it on his wrist, and Clark grabbed his clipboard with the list of names. Then they both followed a moment behind.

Thump!

   Thump!

      Thump!

         Thump!

            Thump!

The boxes landed on the front porch of Great Rapscott School for Girls of Busy Parents.

The teacher poked the first box with her foot.

"Let me out!" came a voice from inside the box.

"Stand back!" Ms. Rapscott warned.

The dogs kept a safe distance.

The headmistress pulled the E-Z open tab with one quick zip and leaped away. A second later, out popped a girl.

"Where am I!?" she hollered.

"You are at Great Rapscott School," Ms. Rapscott replied. "What is your name?"

"Beatrice Chissel!!" Beatrice had been packed wearing a soiled plaid jumper and shirt, the uniform from a previous school that she had been kicked out of some weeks ago. Her short dark hair looked as if she'd cut it herself, her nose was running, and her teeth needed brushing. She didn't smell very good, either.

Lewis checked his watch; it was 7:00 a.m. sharp. Clark put a checkmark next to her name.

"This one's got pluck!" Ms. Rapscott winked at her corgis.

Beatrice Chissel was very small and round, like a beach ball with arms and legs. She narrowed her eyes and gave Ms. Rapscott a suspicious look, then bounced off the porch to take it all in.

She lifted her snub nose and sniffed the salt sea air. She cocked an ear and listened to the racket made by the waves that crashed against large pointy rocks. She felt the sand sting her podgy cheeks like little needles. A clamshell bopped her on the head from a passing seagull and that was it.

Beatrice Chissel climbed back inside her box and pulled the flaps over her head. "Mail me back!!" For once her shrill voice was muffled, which was highly unusual because, for such a young girl, she had developed a set of lungs the size and strength of a professional hog caller.

The reason for this was that no one ever heard Beatrice unless she screamed.

Her parents, Dr. Loulou Chissel and Dr. Lou Chissel, were very busy. They had started out in the cinder-block business and slowly but surely had worked their way up to become prominent cosmetic surgeons. In a stroke of genius Beatrice's father, Dr. Lou Chissel, had even devised a way to fill out wrinkles and lips from the raw materials that he had used to make his cinder blocks.

"It's a win-win situation," Dr. Lou often said.

But the Chissels didn't stop there. Dr. Loulou Chissel had shortened her daughter's name from Beatrice to Bea to save time, because Dr. Chissel was busy experimenting with ways to grow hair on cinder blocks.

"Just think of the possibilities," she crowed.

Dr. Lou rubbed his bald head, "Just think."

As you can imagine, all this thinking required a great deal of quiet. But their daughter, Bea, was always wanting something—like breakfast—and she was always asking questions like, "What's a birthday present?"

When no one answered she would get louder and louder, until she would shriek at a decibel loud enough to shatter glass:

"What's a birthday present?!!!!!!"

This is how Beatrice Chissel became Known for Being Loud.

To keep her quiet Bea's parents made her count cinder blocks, and enter the number in a spiral notebook labeled: NUMBER OF CINDER BLOCKS. So far she had counted 637,523 cinder blocks.

Now she was at Great Rapscott School, and she would not be mailed back home. Instead, in only a matter of hours, Beatrice Chissel would be utterly Lost on Purpose.

29

Chapter 2

MILDRED, FAY, ANNABELLE, AND DAHLIA

*T*here was a distinct snoring sound coming from the second box.

ZI-I-I-I-IP! Ms. Rapscott pulled the E-Z open tab. Sure enough, inside the box Lewis found a student curled up fast asleep. Ms. Rapscott nudged her and leaned over to look inside. "What is your name?"

"Mildred A'Lamode," she said with a mighty yawn.

"OH! This one is *perfect*. Look at her hair!" Ms. Rapscott had a theory that girls with curly red hair were always loaded with enthusiasm.

Mildred had on her favorite pink pajamas with the yellow ducks on them. They were two sizes too small because she'd been wearing them since she was six.

Of course her mother and father were too busy to get her new ones. Mimi and Marcel A'Lamode were a song-and-dance team, as well as internationally acclaimed chefs who were famous for a dish called *les grenouilles et escargots,* which was basically frogs' legs with snails. They had a huge following on their popular TV show where they whipped up French recipes while performing popular French songs like *Frère Jacques.*

Mildred was excited to learn all she could from her parents, but she always got in the way.

"Mon Dieu!" her mother exclaimed when Mildred asked for the thousandth time how to make a cake in the shape of the Eiffel Tower.

"Sacre Bleu!" her father declared. His soufflé was sinking and his flambé was fizzling; he couldn't stop to teach his daughter the lyrics to *Alouette*!

Mimi and Marcel A'Lamode didn't even have

time to show Mildred how to stuff an éclair—they had a lot to do.

Mildred on the other hand had nothing to do, but eventually she did find a hobby . . . something she liked and that she was good at. She watched TV, in her pink pajamas with the yellow ducks on them. She also got to see her parents as much as she wanted—on TV.

This is how Mildred A'Lamode became Known for Being Lazy.

Mildred woke up and stretched. She poked her head out of the box and remembered that she didn't like being outside. The world felt so big, and it made her uneasy. She peeked over the rim and wondered what kind of a place she had landed in where it was normal for a dog to be able to check your name off a list. Mildred wished she was back home in her room—even if she had to eat frogs' legs for the rest of her life.

Ms. Rapscott moved to the third box.

The flaps opened and quick as can be the girl inside tried to hop out, but she caught a toe and fell flat on her face onto the porch.

"What is your name?" The teacher asked as she had the others.

"I'm May Fandrake—I mean I'm Day Frandake—I mean I'm *Fay* Mandrake!"

Fay Mandrake had buckteeth, a small pink nose, and light blond hair, which gave her a sort of rabbity look.

"This one's got a sparkle in her eye." Ms. Rapscott thought that a sparkle in the eye was the sign of an adventurous spirit.

Clark checked her name off the list.

Fay wore a long ragged T-shirt and tights that wouldn't stay up because she had put them on backward.

Her parents were famous for having two sets of octuplets. They were very busy. To keep track of all the babies, they named the first bunch "L" names and the second bunch "N" names. Fay always wanted to help, but she would dress Larry and Lee in pink T-shirts while Laura and Lily would be dressed in blue. She was constantly mixing up Nancy with Noelle, and Nicholas with

Nate. Finally the only thing she was allowed to do was mop the floors.

This is how Fay became Known for Not Being Able to Do Anything Right. Her nose twitched and her eyes darted about nervously. She yanked at her tights and was relieved when everyone's attention shifted to the fourth box.

Lewis waited there for Ms. Rapscott to open it. She pulled the E-Z open tab and a girl with horn-rimmed glasses and long, straight black hair to her waist stepped out. Without having to be asked or offering even a suggestion of a smile she said, "My name is Annabelle Merriweather."

Annabelle wore a pair of running shoes that were five sizes too big and a peanut-butter-and-jelly-stained T-shirt that had been given away free at some sporting event. The shirt hung well below her knees and had a slogan on the front with a smiley face that said: BECAUSE YOU'RE WORTH IT.

"This one is *very* bright," Ms. Rapscott said with authority. "I'll bet you've read the entire *Encyclopedia Britannica*."

Annabelle nodded. She had read the entire *Encyclopedia Britannica* but only because there was nothing else to do. Her mother and father were very busy—they were professional exercisers.

"Your father and I are going out for a run now, dear," Annabelle's mother would say.

"But you just came *in* from a run," Annabelle would complain.

As professional exercisers it was not unusual for the Merriweathers to go out in the morning for a run and not come back for a couple of weeks. Of course they always made sure that their daughter had plenty of peanut butter and jelly to hold her until they returned, but needless to say it wasn't a great arrangement. The Merriweathers were lucky, though, that Annabelle could take care of herself, which is how she became Known for Being Old for Her Age.

Annabelle looked with distaste at the other girls and exhaled loudly through her teeth—a mannerism which she had no doubt picked up from some adult.

There was only one more name on the student

list. Clark stood ready to check "Dahlia Thistle" off. Lewis watched while Ms. Rapscott set to opening the fifth box.

"Oh, dear!" Ms. Rapscott said as she realized there would be no need to open the fifth box. Someone had failed to pull off the kwik-close tape to secure the E-Z shut flaps.

Lewis shook his head sadly, and so did Clark.

"Her mother forgot," Ms. Rapscott sighed. "Probably because she was so busy."

Of all the girls, Dahlia Thistle's family had the distinction of being the busiest. Dahlia's mother wrote a very popular blog about the trials and tribulations of being a mom. This took a lot of her time, but it was difficult because Dahlia was always crying over something like a bad dream, and always badgering her mother to read her a bedtime story.

So Dahlia's mother gave her to her father who was a professional comment writer. He wrote comments on the Internet about toothpaste, shoe-laces, shaving cream, dishwashing detergent, bug spray, slipcovers, you name it.

When he wasn't writing comments, Dahlia's father played miniature golf and participated in Civil War reenactments. He was so busy he gave Dahlia to her grandmother.

It's not that her grandmother didn't love her—it's just that she was busy, too. Dahlia's grandmother was learning Chinese, taking a synchronized swimming class three days a week, and regularly attended seminars in estate planning. She had no time, so she gave Dahlia to her niece Denise, the dog walker. Denise was busy walking dogs, and she was going to school full-time to become a child psychologist, so she had no time for Dahlia either. Denise gave Dahlia to her mother, Dahlia's great-aunt. Dahlia's great-aunt was always on the go too, though, and if she didn't get to meet her friends in the morning to go mall walking, she tended to get cranky.

It became complicated and hard to keep track of where Dahlia Thistle was from one day to the next. As a result she was misplaced more times than a set of keys. She got left by the water fountain in the park, the seventh hole on the miniature golf course, and the food court at the mall, to name but a few.

Everybody was too busy for Dahlia.

"Big girls can take care of themselves and aren't always getting lost, Dahlia," her mother, her father, her grandmother, her grandmother's niece Denise, and her great-aunt said.

But Dahlia was *not* a big girl. In fact she was a very small one because her parents were so busy they'd forgotten to remind her to grow, and she hadn't budged an inch since she was five years old. This is how Dahlia Thistle became Known for Being a Late Bloomer.

Ms. Rapscott shook her head sadly. "Typically, daughters of busy parents can slip down wells, plummet off balconies, or be dragged out to sea, but statistically ninety percent of them simply get . . . lost." The teacher looked through the binoculars again and searched the sky, then abruptly turned on her heel and headed inside.

"Beatrice, Mildred, Fay, and Annabelle, follow me, please!" she called.

"My name's not Beatrice—

it's Bea!" Bea howled as they all shuffled into the schoolroom, except for one. Fay Mandrake lingered. What had happened to Dahlia Thistle? She couldn't stop wondering.

Fay stared at the box, then turned it upside down and shook it. Her eyes grew large when out plopped a ratty-looking, stuffed woolly lamb. She reached down to pick it up and could still feel the warmth from its missing owner. Fay hid the lamb under her shirt and ran to catch up with the others.

Chapter 3
ORIENTATION

All the rooms at Great Rapscott School were round.

Lewis and Clark led Bea, Mildred, Fay, and Annabelle into a classroom. There were books on shelves that went up to the ceiling, a map of the island rolled down like a window shade, a clock on the wall that said 7:31, a chalkboard, paint boxes, crayons, and one large desk that sat in front of five little ones.

A stairway corkscrewed around through the center of the school, and the girls followed the corgis up to the next floor where there was a kitchen. The walls were canary yellow, and on a long wooden table was a birthday cake with pink icing. There were five cabinets, five dinner plates, five soup bowls, five forks and spoons and teacups. Beatrice couldn't help counting them—it was a habit she'd gotten into since she'd started keeping track of her parents' cinder blocks.

Another flight up was the bathroom. It was pink and had five little sinks with five bars of soap. There were five towels and washcloths, five bathrobes, and five pairs of slippers.

"Are we almost there?" Mildred wheezed. She wasn't used to very much activity, outside of watching TV.

But no one paid any attention to her. They wound around up another flight and came out into a dormitory with five beds that were each a different color: blue, green, pink, yellow, and purple.

Ms. Rapscott folded her arms and tapped her foot at the top, waiting for Mildred.

Mildred's cheeks were flaming red, and she was breathing hard. She barely dragged herself up the last step.

"This will not do, Mildred," Ms. Rapscott said, as if she'd never seen such a poor excuse for a girl. "You are a daughter of busy parents. What if they lost you at the Louvre in France and you had to walk to your hotel that was all the way over by the Arc de Triomphe?"

"M-my parents never go to France—they're too busy. C-c-can I," she tried to catch her breath, "sit down?"

Ms. Rapscott paused a moment to consider the request then curtly replied, "No." She motioned for Mildred to stand next to the others, who had been arranged in a line by Lewis.

Bea, Mildred, Fay, and Annabelle sullenly regarded the new teacher, whom they thought wasn't young but wasn't old either. Her hair was coarse but had been tamed into a severe bun. She had a large nose, dark brown horsey eyes, and an oblong face the shape of a cough drop. She had a wiry body inside an oversized thick sweater that a real fisherman could have knitted, and pants the color of mud were shoved into sturdy waterproof boots that were ready for anything. None of the girls thought she was pretty, but she definitely had a sparkle in her eye.

"What's first, Clark?" Ms. Rapscott asked. The dog produced a list of items printed out in order and held them for her to see.

"Hygiene!" She turned to the girls, "Stick out your tongues and say *AHHHH*."

They all complied, as she was very persuasive.

She went down the line and squinted into each one's mouth, but when she got to Bea and tilted the girl's chin up to peer inside, she was shocked. "When was the last time you brushed your teeth?" Ms. Rapscott asked sharply.

Bea couldn't remember, so she thought about kicking the teacher in the shins, but no sooner did the idea flicker through her mind than Ms. Rapscott warned, "I wouldn't if I were you." Something in her tone of voice made Bea think twice. Her kicking leg stayed put, but at that very moment Annabelle Merriweather pointed to Bea and said two little words that would irk the plucky girl and make her want to get even for days to come.

"You stink!" Annabelle held her nose, and the other two girls giggled.

"That'll do, Annabelle." Ms. Rapscott reprimanded the girl with a dark look, and Annabelle's mouth dropped open in surprise, for she wasn't used to being reprimanded, or given dark looks, or even being looked at for that matter.

Meanwhile Bea fumed, trying to decide whether to cut Annabelle Merriweather's hair while she was asleep or pour salt on her oatmeal when she had her back turned. But one thing Bea was sure of, she did not like Ms. Rapscott and would do everything she could to get thrown out of Great Rapscott School for Girls of Busy Parents as soon as possible.

The teacher paced up and down with her arms behind her back like a drill sergeant before his troops. "Hands!" she ordered, and made *Tsk, tsk* sounds as she inspected the four pairs of grimy hands. "It's worse than I thought—but so typical," Ms. Rapscott commented to the corgis. "Their parents are too busy to make them wash!" Clark followed her with his clipboard and wrote down everything she said. "Let's see, tooth brushing . . . hand washing . . . face washing—truly, they all need a good bath, but there's no time for that now. Besides, they're going to be traipsing around in the mud—utterly lost—in only a matter of hours." She made a wave of her hand when she said "utterly lost," as if she'd just said "merrily picnicking." She looked pointedly at a corgi. "You did say it was going to storm, Lewis, correct?"

Lewis nodded crisply.

She paced again. "Then I'd say it's pretty silly to bother with baths."

Clark made a list: Wash faces and hands, brush teeth, silly to bother with baths.

Of course none of this exchange had been lost on Bea, Mildred, Fay, or Annabelle. It was bad enough that they'd been sent here in boxes, like heads of lettuce, that they were at the ends of the earth, in a lighthouse, but traipsing around? Utterly lost? In a storm?

Bea squinched up her face and yelled with all her might. "I'm going to tell my mother!"

"Your mother hardly even notices you're gone, Beatrice." Ms. Rapscott waved a hand dismissively again as she had over "utterly lost." "What's next on the list, Clark?" She looked over his shoulder at the clipboard. "Of course! Bed assignments!"

Bea made a face, but secretly she and Mildred, Fay, and Annabelle had to admit that every single bed was the most perfectly beautiful thing they had ever seen. Canopied and with curtains the girls could pull to make it almost like their own cozy rooms, each one had a headboard carved with curling ocean waves, and the Rapscott school crest in the middle. There was a nightstand with a frilly lamp. All the beds had dust ruffles and under them was a soft rug to put their toes on when they first got up. There were two pillows, crisp white sheets, a puffy quilt, and an extra blanket at the foot, in case they got cold during the night. Best of all, each bed had its own night-light that was plugged in under the nightstand and glowed just enough so that it wasn't pitch dark.

Right away the teacher had Lewis lead a girl to one of the five different colored beds. Bea was put next to the pink bed. "The color of hope, Beatrice!" Ms. Rapscott said.

Mildred was put next to the blue bed. "The color of truth!" Ms. Rapscott exclaimed.

Fay was led to the green bed. "My favorite color!" Ms. Rapscott trilled. "Green: the color of luck, abundance, and asparagus!"

Annabelle was put next to the yellow bed. "The color of wisdom!" Ms. Rapscott intoned. She stood back to see how the girls all looked by their beds, but something was wrong, so she had Lewis move Bea to the blue bed, Mildred to the pink, Fay to yellow, and Annabelle to the purple. But it still wasn't right. The corgi moved the girls around several times, according to Ms. Rapscott's instruction, like pieces on a board game, until Bea was back at the blue bed, Mildred the pink, and Fay stood by the purple, which Ms. Rapscott said was the color of passion and enthusiasm and would do Fay a world of good! Annabelle was then sent to the green bed. The yellow bed would go to Dahlia Thistle—if she was ever found.

"But I don't want the green bed!" Annabelle stamped her foot.

Ms. Rapscott cocked her head and regarded the girl quizzically. "It's not a question of which bed you *want*, Annabelle, it's a matter of which color would do you the most good."

"I hate green!" Annabelle huffed.

"Nevertheless, green will do you the most good, Annabelle." Ms. Rapscott folded her arms in a determined way. "Green. The color of asparagus—delicate, tender, yet perennial—we should all strive to be like the asparagus, girls."

"I don't want to be like an asparagus!" Annabelle marched over to the pink bed. Mildred, not wanting to cause a scene, skittered over to the green bed, which she thought was just as pretty, even though she didn't want to be like an asparagus either.

"Remember there are two sides to everything,

girls." Ms. Rapscott observed the nails on her right hand. "Pink is the color of hope and love, but it can also be foolish and silly."

Foolish and silly? Annabelle could make a peanut butter and jelly sandwich all by herself. She had read the entire *Encyclopedia Britannica* and was probably the *least* foolish or silly person there ever was! She never even laughed out loud if she could help it—which is how it is if you are Old for Your Age. "I don't want the pink bed," she said as seriously as she had ever said anything in her entire life.

"Too late!" Ms. Rapscott exclaimed. "You picked your bed and now you'll have to lie in it!"

Annabelle's eyes filled with tears, but the discussion of bed assignments had officially come to an end. Clark checked it off his list.

Immediately Lewis and Clark trotted down the stairs and reappeared a few moments later with all the boxes which had been flattened.

"And now, girls, comes the best part!" Ms. Rapscott clapped her hands and made a little hop. She smiled broadly for the first time, and the girls noticed she had two front teeth that protruded and noticeably overlapped each other, which gave her a sort of jaunty look. "Boxes and uniforms!"

The corgis proceeded to unfold sides and panels of the very same boxes that the girls had arrived in. The girls watched with amazement and tried to follow the dogs' movements, but it was impossible to keep up. Like a very good magician doing a sleight-of-hand trick, they pushed, pulled, folded, and transformed the boxes in the blink of an eye.

Ms. Rapscott spoke, "Every one of you has your own box. Take care of it: keep it clean, organized, and well-maintained. It will serve as your closet and . . . it will be your only means of transportation home."

Bea, Mildred, Fay, and Annabelle all hesitantly opened the flaps that resembled doors and were surprised to see clothes already hanging.

Ms. Rapscott continued, "Inside you will see your regulation Rapscott uniforms."

"I hate uniforms!" Bea hollered.

"Just the same you will wear it every day that you are here at Great Rapscott School," the teacher said with a casual air.

"No I won't! You can't make me!" Bea yelled.

"Yes I can, Beatrice." Ms. Rapscott's hands were bolted to her narrow hips, and her sturdy booted feet were anchored to the ground in a way that made her appear unstoppable. Of course none of the girls wanted to obey the teacher because they didn't know how. Their parents had all been so busy that they'd never taught their daughters about doing what they were told.

But somehow the girls could not refuse Ms. Rapscott any more than they could stop the earth from turning on its axis or a wave from breaking on the shore.

Soon all four stood before her in their school uniforms. "And please note, girls, you are not allowed to wander any higher in the lighthouse than this floor," she said sternly, and ignored the mumbles of dissent. "Do I make myself clear?"

Bea hoped she'd get kicked out for going to the next floor.

Mildred trembled to think what could be up there.

Fay was far more interested to know where Dahlia Thistle was.

Annabelle thought it was all extremely childish and couldn't care less.

But when the puzzling teacher turned and walked crisply out of the dormitory, the girls scurried after her just to see what she would do next. All except for one. Before she left the room, Fay gently placed the moth-eaten woolly lamb on the yellow bed of wisdom. In the box in front of the bed, a tiny uniform waited for its missing girl.

Chapter 4
How to Find Your Way

"Welcome to the summer term at Great Rapscott School for Girls of Busy Parents!" Ms. Rapscott's words rang out inside the big white lighthouse.

Bea, Mildred, Fay, and Annabelle picked their seats inside the round classroom. Their faces and hands washed, their teeth brushed, they sat in their new navy blue woolen sailor caps and pleated jumpers with thick socks and sensible shoes and looked at each other with various expressions of dislike. One desk remained unoccupied, another disturbing reminder of the missing classmate.

Lewis checked his watch by the large clock that ticked loudly on the wall. It was 8:15 in the morning. Clark busied himself, putting an odd assortment of supplies into five backpacks.

"May I have your attention, please." Ms. Rapscott stood with her hands clasped together. "Beatrice. Mildred. Fay. Annabelle. You have been brought here to Great Rapscott School because your parents are some of the busiest on earth!"

There was a flash of lightning and a rumble of thunder.

The teacher's chin tilted up and her eyes looked down as she spoke. "I was the child of busy parents—just like you. I grew up waiting for a bedtime story, hoping for a hug, and wishing for a birthday cake . . ."

"What's a birthday cake?" Bea yelled.

Annabelle held her ears. "Stop screaming!" Bea stuck her tongue out at Annabelle, and Annabelle exhaled loudly through her teeth.

Ms. Rapscott raised an eyebrow, and the two became quiet and gave each other dirty looks.

"Yes!" the teacher continued, "I was the child of busy parents . . . but I did learn some things that *ordinary* children with parents who are *not* busy do *not* learn. Things like how to make *my own* birthday cake." As if on cue Lewis and Clark entered with the birthday cake the girls had seen earlier in the kitchen. They were each given a slice, complete with ice cream and a lit candle.

"Make a wish, everybody!" Ms. Rapscott said gleefully.

I wish I could get expelled, Bea thought, even though she had to admit the cake, chocolate with strawberry icing, was possibly the best she'd ever tasted. Still, she had been to lots of schools in her short life, starting with pre-pre-pre-pre-school when she was two days old. She had been expelled from all of them, and this would be just like the others.

Mildred gobbled her cake up in three bites—it was definitely better than frogs' legs or anything else her parents made—but she slumped in her chair and anxiously twirled a lock of hair around and around one finger. Her uniform was scratchy, and she wished that she was back in her pajamas with the ducks on them.

Fay ate up the last crumbs and looked down at the floor, which she was relieved to see did not need mopping. She had never even been to school—her parents were homeschooling her, except they never had time to teach her anything. Fay just wished that she wouldn't do too many things wrong.

Annabelle didn't believe in wishes. She finished her cake and dabbed at her lips. She sat with her legs crossed and her lips pursed. The cake was excellent, but she couldn't decide which she hated more, her new school uniform or Beatrice Chissel.

"Mmm delicious!" Ms. Rapscott exclaimed as she finished her cake. Lewis wiped his mouth, and Clark collected the plates.

The wind whistled around the lighthouse and rattled the windows. The room was drafty, and the girls shivered. Lewis glanced at the clock on the wall and synchronized his watch. Ms. Rapscott's fingers rested lightly on her desk, which was clear except for a few textbooks, one of which was: *A Guide to Local Winds and Other Phenomena of Weather.*

"This semester you will be taking a very difficult course." Her face broke into a smile because she loved it when things were very difficult. And just like a teacher would say, "This term you will be learning all about the Revolutionary War," Ms. Rapscott said, "You will be learning all about How to Find Your Way!"

The girls exchanged worried glances.

Ms. Rapscott clapped her hands, and Clark distributed the backpacks.

Here is what was in them:

Official Rapscott rain bonnet

Raincoat

Rain boots

Parachute

Pillow

Slippers

Goggles

Cheese

Crackers

Life vest

Mug

Spoon

Binoculars

Hot chocolate

Thank-you notes

Pencil

Eraser

Beatrice immediately clawed through her pack to look for something that she could use to get herself expelled.

Next to Bea, Mildred went through the contents of her backpack with a growing sense of unease about Great Rapscott School. Why did she need a raincoat, a parachute, goggles, and a life vest if she was taking a course? Besides, it was only 8:30 in the morning, and she was supposed to be fast asleep—in her pajamas. Mildred suddenly panicked. Where were her pink pajamas with the ducks on them? She dug through the backpack. There were slippers . . . but . . . but . . . no pajamas! Mildred moaned softly to herself and raised her hand. "Ms. Rapscott, there are no pajamas."

"Precisely, Mildred," the teacher said tightly. "There are no pajamas."

Mildred was speechless with dread, for what kind of a place was without pajamas? Clark tapped a long pointer against the chalkboard to get everyone's attention.

"Girls!" Ms. Rapscott exclaimed. "In one minute, at exactly nine a.m., the course will begin!"

The girls shifted nervously in their seats.

"You will be graded on the following: pluck, enthusiasm, spirit of adventure, brilliance, and self-reliance. Also as part of the curriculum you will be required to find Dahlia Thistle, who, as you know, is lost."

There was a stunned silence and all that could be heard was the ticktock, ticktock, of the clock. "One more thing . . . if you pass, you may go home for a visit at the end of the semester. Any questions?" Ms. Rapscott asked.

Bea immediately raised her hand. "If we fail do we get kicked out?"

"You will be required to pass the course before you will be allowed to leave the premises," Ms. Rapscott said firmly.

"But what if we *never* pass?" Fay's lower lip started to tremble slightly as she spoke.

"Then you will never leave," Ms. Rapscott said, a little too cheerfully.

Bea's voice rose to a hysterical pitch and her face turned red. **"We won't be allowed to go home? I'm telling my mother!"**

"Your mother is busy, Beatrice. You will be eighteen before she even knows you're gone," Ms. Rapscott replied.

Bea pulled her upper lip down. She had to admit it was probably true.

The others girls sat very still with big eyes.

"Next question?" the teacher said.

Fay raised her hand, "What's pluck?"

Ms. Rapscott snapped a finger. "Dictionary!" she ordered.

Clark zipped across the room and produced the book in a flash.

Ms. Rapscott thumbed through the dictionary muttering, "Hmmm, let's see, plod, plop, plot, ploy . . . PLUCK! 'Courageous readiness to fight or continue against all odds!'"

Fay and the others sat hardly breathing.

Lewis stared at his watch. The clock struck 9:00.

"The course has begun! Good luck!" Ms. Rapscott exclaimed. She strode over to the chalkboard and wrote in big letters:

Question number one.

"The first step for Finding Your Way is what?" There was silence. Ticktock, ticktock, ticktock, the clock ticked away. The teacher searched the group for someone to call on, but no one raised her hand.

"First you must get *what*?" she asked.

Still no one answered.

"Lost!" A gust of wind violently shook the lighthouse as Ms. Rapscott answered for them. "You must get Lost on Purpose, class!"

"But I don't want to get lost!" Beatrice screeched.

"Neither do I!" Fay said, and she thought about the girl missing from the fifth box. "I'm a-fa-fa-fraaaaaaiiiid!" Mildred sobbed, and they all began to cry—even Annabelle, which was surprising being that she was Old for Her Age.

"What if what happened to Dahlia Thistle happens to us?" Fay asked.

"What happened to Dahlia Thistle will undoubtedly happen to you." Ms. Rapscott hurriedly reached for her raincoat. "Which is exactly why you will need to learn How to Find Your Way—and while we're at it we are going to find Dahlia Thistle as well." Ms. Rapscott shoved first one arm then the other into her raincoat. "Now dry your eyes and pull up your socks! And sit up straight, Mildred. A Rapscott Girl never slouches."

Mildred immediately straightened her shoulders and so did all the others, except for Bea who didn't give a hoot about being a Rapscott Girl.

Next Ms. Rapscott tied her rain bonnet securely under her chin. "Rain bonnets on, girls!

Raincoats and boots, too, please, class!" She flung open the door.

"Rain bonnets?" Annabelle looked at hers skeptically.

"I've never even heard of a rain bonnet," Mildred whispered to Fay. Fay had hers on backward. Lewis turned it around and tied it tightly under her chin.

Ms. Rapscott seemed to be in a hurry. "Come with me—a Rapscott Girl never dawdles!"

"You mean OUTSIDE??!!" Mildred said in disbelief.

"But we're only eight years old," cried Fay.

"Going on nine," Annabelle corrected. "I don't want a stupid rain bonnet—I want a coat with a hood!"

"Nothing will do today but a bonnet!" Ms. Rapscott sang out. Cold air surged in through the door as she drove the girls outside.

"You will never be afraid of getting lost if you know how to find your way!" Ms. Rapscott pointed high above them. The beam of light at the top of the Great Rapscott School turned slowly 360 degrees, shining against the leaden gray sky.

"You can see it for miles," she exclaimed. "All you have to do is look!"

Chapter 5

THE SKYSWEEPER WINDS

"Question number two!" Ms. Rapscott announced as she led the girls down the walk of the school. "How do you Get Lost on Purpose, class?" Ms. Rapscott asked.

The wind was blowing fiercely, and the girls held onto their Rapscott rain bonnets with both hands. But no one answered.

"Never bring a *what*?" she asked.

There was still no answer.

Ms. Rapscott sighed. "Never bring a—starts with an *m* and is three letters?"

"Mop! Mop!" Fay called out. "Never bring a mop!"

Annabelle rolled her eyes.

Ms. Rapscott snapped her fingers again, and Lewis trotted to her carrying a large rolled-up paper. "Never bring a *map*!" He dropped it into her hands, and she tore it up into tiny little pieces. The girls gasped as the bits of map blew over the cliff and out to sea.

"Now then, class." Ms. Rapscott looked as if she was about to make a special announcement. "Mittens are in your pockets. You will need them for the higher altitudes!"

"H-Higher altitudes?" Mildred stammered.

"Parachutes out, class!" Ms. Rapscott commanded, and wriggled into hers as did Lewis and Clark. She pointed to a long tab. "Always remember, pull this tab by your left shoulders to open the chutes, girls—or else you will fall from the sky and get squashed onto the ground."

"My parents are not going to be happy!" It was 9:10 and Mildred was supposed to be home snug in bed wearing pajamas—not a parachute.

"Your parents are busy, Mildred, and probably wouldn't even notice if you *were* squashed onto the ground," Ms. Rapscott replied.

"But Ms. Rapscott—" Mildred wanted to go home—now.

"**Parachutes out!**" she called. "Quickly! Quickly!"

Against their will Bea, Mildred, Fay, and Annabelle were soon grappling with belts and straps and complicated buckles. Lewis and Clark checked and rechecked each student, paying special attention to Fay.

Ms. Rapscott cupped her ear in one hand. "Do you hear it?"

"Hear what?" Bea screamed.

"**SHHHHHHSH!**" Ms. Rapscott scolded. "The Skysweeper Winds are coming—get ready, girls."

"**Get ready for what?!**" Bea yelled even louder.

There was a sound now like a locomotive off in the distance but getting closer all the time.

Lewis and Clark got into position beside Ms. Rapscott and waited.

"Here they come!" Ms. Rapscott cried.

"**What are Skysweeper Winds?**"

Bea yelled even louder, but now the noise was so loud that it drowned out even Bea's voice.

The Skysweeper Winds, known only to those parts, suddenly blew so hard that Bea had to hold on to Fay, who held on to Mildred, who held on to Annabelle, who held on to the Great Rapscott School signpost.

WHOOOOOOSH!!!! The next gust picked them right up off the ground and sent them aloft, flying over the lighthouse, circling around like a flock of seagulls.

Ms. Rapscott sailed by and shouted, "Follow me, girls!" Not that they really had a choice since the wind kept them right behind her.

"I know this road by heart," Ms. Rapscott said confidently. It snaked along the cliff, and they flew right over it.

Below the mailman called out, "Hello, Ms. Rapscott!"

"Say hello, girls," Ms. Rapscott ordered. "A Rapscott Girl is always polite." But before they could utter a word, they were already fifty yards past him.

As you can imagine Bea, Mildred, Fay, and Annabelle were terrified, somersaulting through the air like so many leaves in the breeze. They could see forever, but they couldn't stop thinking about falling from the sky and getting squashed onto the ground. Below, boats and ships in the harbor looked like toys. It was a long, long way to fall.

Lots of people waved. Mildred wondered again what kind of a place she had come to where it was normal to see children blowing about like confetti.

The girls followed along the coastline. Behind them the beacon from the lighthouse became farther away with every blink. Then the Skysweeper Winds changed direction and turned them inland. They seemed to be flying over a new road. Off to their left Great Rapscott was fading fast.

"I know this road like the back of my hand," Ms. Rapscott said with certainty.

There were less people and cars about, and the lighthouse flashed one last time before it was swallowed up by the horizon. The girls could see the practicality of their rain bonnets now, for the wind blew so ferociously nothing else would have stayed on their heads. They flew in a group behind the teacher. She had her binoculars out and peered through them often.

Bea, Mildred, Fay, and Annabelle were carried between towers of pink and gold sculpted clouds hundreds of stories high. Below, the road was just one lane. Like a ribbon of white, it rolled forever over hills, past farms, houses, and churches with tall steeples as far as the eye could see.

The longer they were carried by the winds the more comfortable Bea and Fay became, being the more adventurous of the group. But Mildred now knew why she never left her bedroom—peculiar things could happen to you outside. Annabelle had never read a thing about this in the *Encyclopedia Britannica*, and she was simply outraged.

"Mittens out, class!" Ms. Rapscott called. The wind had switched direction, spinning the girls around in a dizzying circle, and when they had straightened out they were blowing over yet a different road.

Each girl found the mittens that were in her pockets just as a mass of dark clouds blanketed the sky. There were no more farms, or cars, or houses. Tall dreary pine trees lined the road, and crows joined them in the sky, cawing nastily at the girls.

Bea waved her arms at them and cawed back.

Below was just a narrow lane of dirt and weeds, but now they were so far up they could barely see it. The wind was taking them higher and higher. It whistled in their ears, blew inside their collars, and sent chills all the way down their spines, right into their regulation Rapscott boots. By now it had collected all sorts of things, too: paper clips, a tennis ball, some buttons, loose change, a starfish, pinecones, and a little girl.

She was wearing lime-green tights and a yellow ruffled skirt and top. Her sparse gold hair, the color of dandelions, flew straight back from her fragile birdlike face. She was very tiny and traveling feetfirst at a tremendous speed when Ms. Rapscott reached out and grabbed hold of one of her arms.

"My name is Ms. Rapscott. What is your name?" the teacher asked.

"Dahlia Thithle," the girl lisped.

"This-s-s-s-s-tle." Ms. Rapscott drew her lips back from her teeth and carefully pronounced the *s*. "A Rapscott Girl always enun-ci-ates, Dahlia. Now say, This-s-s-s-stle."

"I can't," called Dahlia. "I'm a Late Bloomer." The tiny girl gripped Ms. Rapscott's sleeve with all her might. "Where ith Great Rapthcot Thcool for Girlth?"

"You can see it for miles! Just look for the light!" Ms. Rapscott shouted back. Lewis and Clark managed to blow over to Dahlia and handed her the fifth backpack they had brought along, just in case. They even got her into her parachute, and thankfully the weight slowed her down so that she was soon flying along at their speed— but Ms. Rapscott dared not let go.

"Hold on!" Bea yelled to the teacher.

"Don't let go of her!" Mildred and Annabelle cried.

"I found your lamb!" Fay called to Dahlia.

Dahlia thanked Fay and said, "Tell him that I'm fine!" She was light as a feather and had to shout to be heard over the wind that pulled her with ferocious force.

The teacher pointed to the long tab by her left shoulder. "You can pull this to open the chute!"

Dahlia reached for the tab. Beatrice, Mildred, Fay, and Annabelle gasped.

"Not now!" They all yelled.

But it was too late. The chute opened with a *WHOOOOSH!* The wind caught it like a sail, and Dahlia Thistle blew away. "He-e-e-l-l-l-l-p!" she screamed.

The others watched in horror as the small girl disappeared.

Ms. Rapscott searched the sky with her binoculars.

But Dahlia Thistle had been carried away by the Skysweeper Winds.

Chapter 6
LESS TRAVELED ROAD

"There she is!" Off in the distance Ms. Rapscott could see the little girl floating down to earth. "Locate the tab on your chutes, girls, and prepare yourselves for landing!"

Sure enough the winds began to die down.

"I'm falling!" Mildred cried.

"Open your chutes, class!" Ms. Rapscott ordered.

All the girls found the tab except for Fay, who mistakenly pulled on her zipper. Luckily Lewis opened her chute as he whizzed by or Fay would have been squashed onto the ground as so often happens to girls of busy parents.

Bea, Mildred, Fay, and Annabelle had surprisingly soft landings. They picked themselves up, and dusted themselves off, relieved that they were still all in one piece.

Lewis checked his watch, and it was 10:55.

"Binoculars out, class!" Ms. Rapscott ordered. She peered through hers and a moment later whooped, "Dahlia Thistle has made a perfect touchdown!"

"Is she all right?" Fay asked anxiously.

"She is quite fine." Then Ms. Rapscott asked, "Question number three! Do you know where you are?" The girls looked from one to the other. "Beatrice? Mildred? Fay? Annabelle?"

"NO!" Bea screamed, determined to make herself as unpleasant as possible to get expelled as soon as she could.

"Correct!" the teacher said to the surprise of the others, especially Bea. "Since none of you know where you are, I am happy to report that you are officially, hopelessly Lost on Purpose!"

Before them was a rickety-looking signpost that said: LESS TRAVELED ROAD. It certainly looked less traveled; it was nothing but a dirt lane made up of two tracks with a ridge of weeds down the center. One way went back in the direction from which they came and the other way disappeared into a thick forest of fir trees.

Ms. Rapscott cleared her throat ceremoniously. "Question number four!" The sky darkened even more than it already had been, and it looked like it would storm any minute. "Which way should we go, class?"

Annabelle rolled her eyes, "That's easy, we should go back the way we came."

"Incorrect!" Ms. Rapscott said to the delight of Bea and the surprise of everyone else, especially Annabelle. "Unfortunately, going back the way we came will take several years."

"SEVERAL YEARS?!" Annabelle sputtered.

"Don't sputter, Annabelle, it will give you the hiccups," Ms. Rapscott said. A large drop of rain plopped onto her bonnet, then another, then another. "The Skysweeper Winds only blow north, and we would have to walk hundreds of miles the entire way home."

Ms. Rapscott gave the girls a nod and turned on her heel.

"But what about Dahlia Thistle?" Fay cried. "Shouldn't we try to find her?"

"Impossible!" Ms. Rapscott's coat flapped jauntily behind her as she took off with Lewis and Clark up Less Traveled Road and into the fir forest. "We will have to wait, girls!"

"For what?" They all trotted to keep up with the teacher.

"A full moon and a high tide!" Ms. Rapscott sang out. "Isn't it thrilling?"

None of the girls thought so.

Bea just wanted to go home, but she knew her only hope was to pass the course. It made her want to scream.

Fay couldn't stop worrying about Dahlia Thistle.

Annabelle was still burned up that she had answered question number four wrong and thought it wasn't fair—especially since Bea had gotten question number three right by mistake.

Bea couldn't help feeling a glimmer of pride that she had answered right and know-it-all Annabelle had answered wrong. *"Who stinks now?"* Bea thought, and grinned to herself.

Mildred huffed and puffed. She was way behind the others and wished she was more like them.

Bea stopped to wait for Mildred. "HURRY UP!" she bellowed.

"I-I'm com-ing!" Mildred panted. She wasn't used to so much exercise; in fact she wasn't used to *any* exercise. It was now 12:00. Every single day at 12:00 she watched her parents on TV— in her pajamas. Mildred's eyes welled up with tears, and she felt very sorry for herself. Not only did she not have the pajamas with the ducks on them, now she had no pajamas at all. She wanted to go home. She did not want to end up like that Dahlia girl, lost for good.

When Mildred finally caught up to Bea, Fay, and Annabelle, they continued on a little slower, and this put them all in even fouler moods. At this point the girls could have found comfort in one another's company, but their parents were so busy they'd never had the time to teach their daughters How to Get Along with Others, and so Bea, Fay, Mildred, and Annabelle didn't know how. They walked in silence, thinking dark thoughts about Ms. Rapscott and wishing that they were home counting cinder blocks, watching TV, mopping floors, or reading the encyclopedia instead of stuck with each other on Less Traveled Road.

They walked and walked and walked without speaking. They stopped to eat their crackers and cheese without exchanging a word. They looked at the scenery that was monotonously covered in fir trees. By the time Beatrice Chissel had finished her last cracker, the novelty of actually answering a question correctly in a school had worn off. In its place two words taunted her and began to repeat in her ears with each step: you stink . . . you stink . . . you stink . . . until she couldn't take it anymore and yelled at Annabelle, "YOU STINK!"

"I do not!" Annabelle yelled back.

"You do, too!" Bea yelled louder. "I'll bet your parents aren't even all that busy!"

"I'll bet they are." Annabelle flicked her long hair angrily over her shoulder.

"I'll bet my parents are busier than yours!" Bea snapped.

"Sometimes my parents go for a run and don't come home for two weeks," Annabelle replied coldly.

"That's impossible!" Bea scoffed. "Nobody can run for two weeks straight."

"Two weeks? Are you kidding?" Annabelle waved her hand as if to say two weeks was nothing. "But I can take care of myself."

Mildred stuck out her chin. "My parents have their own TV show. They're internationally acclaimed chefs! Everything they make is very French and very complicated and very delicious."

"But you don't ever get to see them," Fay reminded her, for she never got to see her parents.

"Yes, I do! All the time!" Mildred insisted, and then she frowned. "On TV."

"My mother just had octuplets," Fay bragged. "For the second time!"

Annabelle exhaled loudly through her teeth as she made the calculations quickly in her head, "You mean you have *sixteen* brothers and sisters?"

"Yes," Fay said. "And they are all either L's or N's. Laura, Lily, Larry, Lee, Lorraine, Lane, Langston, and Lola. Then there's Nancy, Ned, Noelle, Nicholas, Nadia, Nate, Neil, and Natalie.

"But you're not an *L* or an *N*!" the others all said.

"I know," Fay looked down. "My parents named me before they got busy."

Suddenly there was a loud crack of thunder, and the girls jumped. It had been raining but by the time Bea, Mildred, Fay, and Annabelle reached Ms. Rapscott and the dogs it was pouring. Mud sucked at the girls' boots and their mittens were soon soaked through.

The rain beat down all around them now. It streamed off their bonnets, squiggled down their raincoats, and pooled around their sturdy Rapscott boots. Their socks were soggy, they were shivering with cold, and it was getting dark. They were hungry, hopelessly lost, sinking in the mud up to their ankles, and to top it all off they could not go back the way they came.

Chapter 7
THE BUMBERSHOOT TREE

Ms. Rapscott stood with her head back, torrents of rain streaming off her face, because besides heaps of snow there was nothing she loved more than torrents of rain. "Jolly good luck!" she exclaimed to the corgis, smiling broadly, for she had spotted just the thing for the girls.

"Question number five! What is the name of that tree?" Ms. Rapscott pointed to an unusual-looking fir tree. It had a little chimney on one side and bushy branches that curved out in the shape of a gigantic umbrella.

Annabelle had had enough! She balled up her hands into fists and stamped her foot, splashing the others, who jumped back. "What does this tree have to do with finding our way? I thought you were going to teach us rules, and steps, and tips, and plans!" Annabelle loved rules, and steps, and plans.

"Annabelle, rules and steps and tips and plans will make you old before your time," Ms. Rapscott said sternly.

Annabelle's mouth fell open and then snapped shut. She glared at her classmates, daring them to giggle.

Lewis checked his watch; it was 3:30.

"This is a Bumbershoot Tree!" Ms. Rapscott swept back a curtain of low branches. "The perfect place to camp when One Is Lost on Purpose." With that, she ducked her head and disappeared inside the little tree.

The plucky girl, Bea, was the first one to follow the teacher.

Quick as bunnies the other girls scurried in behind her and were surprised to see that under the Bumbershoot Tree it was warm and dry. Pine needles covered the floor and made it soft and springy. There was a good-sized couch, a lamp, and even a small hearth with a kettle filled with water, as if it were just waiting for cold weary travelers. Lewis switched the light on, and Clark had a merry fire burning in no time.

"Socks off! Slippers on!" Ms. Rapscott instructed the girls to place their wet things by the fire. "Blankets and pillows out, please!"

Soon the girls were comfortably seated on the couch, leaning up against their pillows, snug in their blankets.

"It looks like someone lives here," Mildred said.

"Someone does," Ms. Rapscott replied. "Bumbershoots are very hospitable creatures. They offer shelter to those in need and all they ask in return is a thank-you note."

"What's a thank-you note?" Bea wanted to know and so did Mildred, Fay, and even Annabelle, because their parents had always been too busy to teach them about such things.

"Just tell the Bumbershoot why you are thankful to be able to sit under his tree," Ms. Rapscott said. "In plain language . . . not too flowery or it will sound insincere. A Rapscott Girl is always sincere, girls."

The girls found the note cards and now they knew why they'd been included in their backpacks.

While the girls were writing, Ms. Rapscott took out a variety of sandwiches. She brought her favorite, tomato on rye with lots of lettuce and mustard. Lewis and Clark liked egg salad with a dash of green pepper and watercress with the crust cut off their bread. There were turkey sandwiches on rolls, ham sandwiches on whole wheat, chicken salad sandwiches on croissants, and even peanut butter and jelly sandwiches on white bread for Annabelle, to make her feel at home. There were gherkin pickles and birthday cake for dessert. When everything was set out, Ms. Rapscott leaned over to read Annabelle's note which said:

Dearest Mr. Bumbershoot (which means "umbrella" in England because I read it in the Encyclopedia Britannica),

Thank you ever so much for the use of your fabulous tree! It is extremely magnificent of you. I will treasure the experience for as long as I live.

"No gushing, please, Annabelle." Ms. Rapscott handed the note back.

Annabelle sighed. She erased and started over.

Ms. Rapscott read Bea's thank-you note.

DEAR BUMBERSHOOT!

WHEN I FIRST SAW THIS TREE I THOUGHT IT WAS JUST ANOTHER WEIRDO RAPSCOTT SCHOOL THING, LIKE GETTING LOST ON PURPOSE. UGH!! OR WEARING A STUPID BONNET. YUCK!! BUT IT WAS THE ENTIRE OPPOSITE!!!!! IF IT WEREN'T FOR YOUR TREE WE'D STILL BE IN THE MUD. EW!!!!!

I MEAN THIS SINCERELY!!!!!!!!!
BEATRICE CHISSEL

Ms. Rapscott handed the note back to Bea and said loudly, "TOO! MANY!! EXCLAMA-TION!!! POINTS!!!! Beatrice!!!!!"

Bea put her hands over her ears, "All right," she said softly, and then got back to work.

Ms. Rapscott next picked up Fay's note and had to squint to read it.

> Dear Mr. ~~Bumboshirt~~ Bloomerchop, Chimneychute,
>
> Thank you for leting us stay under your tree. In our class a girl got lost—I fond her lam. If you see her tell her we are looking for her. She is about for feet tall high with blon hair. I hope she finds a tree.

"You must write larger, Fay, larger. A Rapscott Girl is always bold." The teacher corrected all the misspellings with a red pencil and handed the note back to Fay to rewrite.

The last note that Ms. Rapscott read was Mildred's:

> Dear Bumbershoot,
> Thanks for letting us stay under your tree. It is very nice here. Could you get a TV? It would be even better with a TV.

Ms. Rapscott handed the note back for revision. "Very good, Mildred, except for the part about the TV."

"But that's the whole thank-you note," Mildred moaned.

Ms. Rapscott would hear none of it. "Start again!"

There were changes, corrections in spelling, and penmanship until finally Ms. Rapscott was satisfied that all the thank-you notes were perfect. "There." She propped them up in a line on the mantel.

Next she asked the class to please take out their mugs, spoons, and packets of instant hot chocolate. By now the kettle was boiling, and she filled their cups.

Lewis and Clark ate their sandwiches and then warmed their paws by the fire.

Ms. Rapscott sat on the chair with her stocking feet on an upholstered ottoman. She dabbed at her lips with a napkin.

"Question number six!" she said.

"How many of you know how to ride a bike? Sew on a button? Hammer a nail?"

The girls stared at the teacher with blank expressions because none of them knew how to do any of those things.

"Just as I suspected," she said thoughtfully. "Here at Great Rapscott School you will learn things that your parents are too busy to teach you."

"What sorts of things?" Fay asked.

"Things like how to make toast, say please and thank you, and ice-skate."

Lewis and Clark looked up and nodded. The girls had all eaten their sandwiches and were starting on their birthday cake.

Ms. Rapscott ate the part of her cake with the most icing first. She chewed thoughtfully. "When I was your age my parents were *very* busy just like yours." The rain continued pattering against the Bumbershoot Tree, and the wind rocked the branches every now and then, but the girls stayed warm and dry with their blankets wrapped around them.

Mildred raised her hand. "If your parents were so busy, how did you learn to do stuff?"

"It all started one Thanksgiving Day many, many years ago," Ms. Rapscott said wistfully.

The fire popped, and the girls settled back to listen.

"My parents were important scientists and were always off to the farthest corners of the earth studying all matter of flora and fauna. While they were busy I lived in the room at the top of our house that had windows on three sides. I called it my lookout tower, and it was from up there that I watched and waited for my parents to return.

"Did they?" Fay asked.

"Seldom. I had to learn to rely on myself." Ms. Rapscott pursed her lips and gave the class a side-long look, as if she thought the girls should do the same. "It was Thanksgiving Day and I was cooking *my own* turkey. The table was set, and the turkey was cooked just right. I ate and ate and was just starting to feel full when I noticed . . ." Ms. Rapscott stopped for moment here to go through her backpack. She held up something for the class to see. "Question number seven! Who can tell me what this is?"

"It looks like a stupid old chicken bone!" Bea shouted.

"Incorrect!" Ms. Rapscott waved the bone in the air. "Anybody? Fay, Mildred, Annabelle?"

"Can I see?" Mildred asked, and the teacher placed it in her hands. Mildred turned it over a few times and held it up to the light. For a split second, and if none of the girls blinked, they would have seen it sparkle. "Wow," Mildred whispered.

"It's a *wish*bone," Ms. Rapscott said.

The girls sat, their eyes wide with amazement, except for Annabelle who was far too grown-up to believe in such things.

"What'd you wish for?" Bea asked, and she even forgot to say it loudly.

"I wished that I was with my parents. To my astonishment, the wish came true. Soon I was with my parents in a deep dark jungle, and they were busy studying strange plants. I couldn't believe my luck."

"Then what happened?" Mildred wanted to know.

"Well . . . they were glad to see me at first." Ms.

Rapscott exhaled deeply. "But soon they were so busy, they hardly even noticed that I was there."

"It's always that way," Annabelle grumbled, and so did the others.

"While they were busy I wandered off deeper and deeper into the jungle. I became utterly lost. I called for my parents, but they didn't answer. I had no food and no water and I was *very* afraid."

"The bone! The bone!" the girls all talked at once. "Did you still have it? Where was it? Did it have any wishes left?"

"I still had the bone." Ms. Rapscott spoke quickly now. "But of course, I didn't know if it had any more wishes left, and if it did, I needed to think long and hard about what I wanted to wish for."

"I'd wish to go back to my parents," Mildred suggested.

"My parents were busy, Mildred," Ms. Rapscott replied.

"Oh yeah, that's right," the chubby red-haired girl said sadly.

"I'd wish to go back home," Annabelle said astutely.

"There was nothing for me to do at home except wait for my parents."

Annabelle nodded. She knew the feeling.

"No, I knew I needed to rely on *myself*!" Ms. Rapscott popped the last of the cake into her mouth for emphasis. "So I thought and thought and thought. I started to imagine where I wanted to *be* if I could be anywhere, and what I wanted to *do* if I could do anything. I imagined an exciting place by the sea with storms, and hurricanes, and blizzards that lasted for weeks on end."

"In the center of all this I imagined instead of a lookout tower—a lighthouse—with the wind and rain and snow and the waves pounding all around but unable to damage it no matter what! I imagined my days filled with time to explore or to not be busy at all and dream all day if I wanted to. My nights I imagined being in my lighthouse safe and warm. I imagined that I could watch and study everything from there. And then eventually I could teach other girls of busy parents everything that I had learned."

"So you made the wish," Bea said.

"I made the wish," Ms. Rapscott replied.

"And it all came true," Mildred said.

"It all came true."

"And here we are," Fay said.

"And here you are."

Annabelle didn't know what to think anymore. "But what about the wishbone? Can you still wish for anything you want?"

"All wishbones are the same, Annabelle, they offer three wishes. I had used two. There was one last wish." Ms. Rapscott would say no more, and when the girls asked her what she wished for, she just smiled mysteriously but still wouldn't tell them.

Chapter 8

THE TOP OF THE BIRTHDAY CAKE

Bea woke up the next morning with a start and shouted, "637,524!"

For a moment Mildred thought she was still home, too. She felt around for the TV remote and couldn't figure out why it wasn't under her pillow where she always kept it.

Fay was surprised to see that she wasn't still under the Bumbershoot Tree, which is where she could have sworn she was when she fell asleep.

Annabelle sat up in her pink bed in a dither. "We're back at the school!"

It was true. They were lying in the beds they had been assigned to, what seemed like ages ago but was really just the morning before.

"Humph!" Annabelle muttered under her breath as she picked at the pink quilt. "We'll just see who's foolish and silly."

Mildred peeked at herself under the covers and was dismayed to find that she was dressed in Rapscott underwear. It was lovely under-wear mind you—white with navy blue stitch-ing and the school crest embroidered in white on the shirt—still, it wasn't her pink pajamas with the ducks on them, and she had the same sinking feeling that she'd had yesterday when she'd arrived, only worse.

"How did we get *here*?" Bea wondered aloud. Of course none of the other girls knew either.

It was odd.

Lewis arrived with four cups of hot choco-late and Clark with four bowls of ice cream and birthday cake. This was definitely an improve-ment over what they usually got for breakfast at home. Still, when the candles were lit, the girls all wished for the same thing: that they could be packed up in their boxes and sent home this very day.

Ms. Rapscott sailed into the room. "Good morning, girls!" she sang out cheerfully. "I trust you all slept as snug as bugs in rugs!" Without waiting for an answer, she turned to one of her dogs. "What's on the list, Clark?" She leaned over to get a look at his clipboard, which by now, the girls assumed he carried with him wherever he went. "Let's see . . . wake up, eat ice cream and birthday cake . . . well you've already accomplished that! Check it off, Clark, check it off!"

Clark checked it off.

"I do so *love* to check things off lists; it gives one such a feeling of accomplishment," the teacher trilled. "A Rapscott Girl always gets much done in a day, girls! Now let's see, take a bath . . . brush teeth . . . dress . . . *meeting*." Her eyes lit up at the idea of the meeting.

Not knowing what happened at a *meeting* but sure it couldn't be good, Bea scowled, Mildred closed her eyes tightly, Fay put the covers over her head, and Annabelle exhaled loudly through her teeth.

"You have exactly one hour to take a bath, brush your teeth, and dress in your uniforms before you are to gather in the schoolroom for our *meeting*."

Ms. Rapscott and Lewis and Clark left the girls to get busy right away with their list of things to do.

The morning light was just beginning to shine through the windows and Mildred tried to remark encouragingly, "At least it's not raining," but none of the others seemed to care. Great Rapscott was such an odd place—rain or shine.

The girls took their baths and brushed their teeth. When they looked inside their boxes, they were surprised to see fresh uniforms. Even their mud-caked boots from the day before were sparkling clean.

It was very odd indeed.

At 8:00 sharp Bea, Mildred, Fay, and Annabelle

were all sitting at their desks, full of questions. How had they ended up back at the school when they'd gone to sleep in the Bumbershoot Tree? Was it magic? Here in the classroom on a sunny morning it seemed like it all could have been a dream.

But Ms. Rapscott seemed to ask more questions than she answered. "May I have your attention, please!" The chalkboard was filled with a drawing of a cake with five tiers that got smaller toward the top. On each tier a piece of paper covered something. What could it mean?

Ms. Rapscott spoke. "Yesterday you all did very well, class. But some of you did better than others." Lewis stood off to one side. Clark was by the chalkboard, pointer in hand. They both nodded in agreement.

"Beatrice. Mildred. Fay. Annabelle. Life is like trying to bake your own birthday cake without a recipe!" Ms. Rapscott looked off into space, as if she were recalling some distant past. "When I was your age I tried to bake my own birthday cake with all kinds of ingredients: sugar, vinegar, pepper, eggs, mustard, flour, ketchup, and butter,

117

but because I didn't have a recipe, I ended up with some awful cakes. I never gave up trying to find out what worked, though." She paused here to ponder, and Clark tapped the chalkboard a few times.

"Ahem." Ms. Rapscott patted her bun and repeated, "Yes, life is like trying to bake your own birthday cake without a recipe, girls!"

Fay raised her hand. "I don't get it."

Ms. Rapscott waved for silence. "As you can see the drawing of the birthday cake is divided into five sections. Whoever is at the top of the cake has done an excellent job and will get to be Head Girl for the week."

Bea suspected she was at the bottom of the cake; Mildred figured she was at the bottom of the cake; Fay knew for sure she was at the bottom of the cake; and Annabelle was confident she was at the very top of the cake.

Ms. Rapscott nodded to Clark and swiped off the sheet of paper at the bottom of the cake. "Dahlia Thistle. She's not here. That's where you end up. I can't blame her—but I can't put her on the top of the cake either."

The only sound that could be heard was from the large clock. The girls held their breath as Ms. Rapscott revealed the name under the next paper.

"Mildred," she said. "You are next to the bottom on the birthday cake." Mildred looked down at the floor. Ms. Rapscott spoke sternly. "You lagged behind all day, Mildred. You need to get stronger, but you do have lots of enthusiasm. If you try harder I am sure you will be higher on the cake next week."

"We have to do this again next week?" Mildred said weakly, and even her curly red hair seemed to lose some of its spring.

"Yes, every week here you have the chance to be on top of the cake," Ms. Rapscott said merrily, for she loved the idea of self-improvement. "Next up the cake!" Ms. Rapscott announced and ripped away the third sheet of paper. "Annabelle!"

Annabelle sighed and pushed her glasses up her nose.

"Annabelle, you show a great deal of promise and are very self-reliant, but you could use a bit of Mildred's enthusiasm."

Annabelle sighed again.

"—and less sighing," Ms. Rapscott added. "Next up the cake is—" She pulled the fourth paper off. "Fay!"

Fay made a sound that was a cross between a squeak and a squeal. She couldn't believe that not only was she not at the bottom of the cake, she was almost all the way to the top. "Fay, you performed strongly. Yesterday you kept up right behind Beatrice, and you never complained. You should be proud."

Fay grinned. Her buckteeth stuck out, and her light hair hung limply, but she had two dots of pink on her cheeks which greatly improved her looks.

Annabelle raised her hand to speak and said, "This isn't fair—Bea was loud all day long—and she complained about the uniforms!"

"This *is* fair, Annabelle, and furthermore a Rapscott Girl is always a good sport." Ms. Rapscott stared at Annabelle Merriweather, and Annabelle Merriweather stared right back at Ms. Rapscott until finally it was Annabelle who blinked first, because nobody in the world can win a staring contest with Ms. Rapscott. She continued, "At the top of the cake is"—with a flick of the wrist she removed the last covering—"Beatrice!"

No one said a word. For the first time since she'd come to Great Rapscott School, Bea's face broke into a wide grin. She hadn't been this happy since she got kicked out of her last school for putting mashed potatoes that she saved from dinner in the headmistress's penny loafers.

Ms. Rapscott explained, "Beatrice, you led the entire way yesterday. You were the only one to answer a question correctly. Outstanding job."

Lewis and Clark stepped forward to shake her hand.

"Now Beatrice will be Head Girl for the rest of the week!" Ms. Rapscott exclaimed.

"But Ms. Rapscott! Ms. *Rapscott*!" Fay waved her hand furiously and was finally allowed to speak. "How did we ever get from the Bumbershoot Tree yesterday to here?"

"Bumbershoot Tree?" Ms. Rapscott said incredulously.

"The tree we were inside yesterday . . . after . . .

we flew on the . . . Skysweeper Winds," Fay said a little hesitantly, for she was always getting things mixed up and now she wasn't so sure.

"I never heard of such a thing. Lewis? Clark? Have you ever heard of such a thing?" The dogs both shook their heads vehemently.

"When we flew!!!" the other three girls chimed in at once.

"Flew?" she huffed. "We have much to accomplish today, and you are all being silly."

The girls looked from one to the other, none of them silly enough—especially Annabelle—to argue with Ms. Rapscott.

But there was one thing Fay wasn't mixed up about and that was the lost girl. "What about Dahlia Thistle? Aren't we going to go find her?"

"We need to wait, Fay," Ms. Rapscott answered firmly. "I told you before."

"For a full moon?" the girl said.

"And a high tide," the teacher answered.

Chapter 9

Ms. Rapscott's Girls' Routine

Every day Ms. Rapscott's girls had to be washed, dressed in their uniforms, and ready to go down to the classroom to attend Morning Meeting by 8:00 sharp, where they had ice cream and birthday cake.

Ms. Rapscott always had an inspiring remark for the day, like this one: "Remember, class, we must all strive to be like a good pair of boots: sturdy, durable, and waterproof. A Rapscott Girl is always waterproof!" As Head Girl, Bea got to write all the remarks down on the chalkboard.

At Morning Meeting, Lewis timed the girls for

exactly one minute, so they could voice any complaints or wishes they had.

Annabelle always had lots of complaints: "Mildred snores, Bea didn't wash her hands after she used the bathroom, Fay talks in her sleep, my socks itch, my shoes squeak—"

Lewis would give the signal, and Ms. Rapscott would exclaim, "Time's up! Next!"

"I wish Annabelle would stop complaining," Bea said on more than one occasion.

"I wish I had my pink pajamas with the ducks on them," Mildred said practically every day.

"I wish we could find Dahlia Thistle," Fay said, worried about the lost girl. Where could she be?

"When the moon is full and the tide is high we will look," Ms. Rapscott would always reply.

Morning Meeting was also the time for the girls to be given letters and packages from home, if there were any, but usually there weren't. In fact, since Bea, Mildred, Fay, Annabelle, and Dahlia had left, their parents were busier than ever.

Bea's father, Dr. Lou Chissel, had invested in

a dump truck full of spackle paste as an obvious addition to his cinder-block business. Bea's mother, Dr. Loulou Chissel, had worked day and night to find a way to use the stuff in her new line of makeup as a sunblock. This is why at Morning Meeting Bea never heard from her parents, except for once when she received a Box-o-Fun from a company that specialized in sending packages to kids of busy parents away at camp. In it was a sports water bottle that smelled like garden mulch, some Band-Aids, a car-sickness bag, and three cookies shrink-wrapped in plastic that were as hard as cinder blocks. The only thing that made Bea feel better was when Mildred received an envelope from her parents with nothing inside of it. They had forgotten to include the letter.

But who could blame Mildred's parents? With their daughter away, the A'Lamodes had finally taken that trip to France and were about to go into production for the French version of their TV show, where they cooked American food, sang country-western songs, and square-danced

all at the same time. Since Mildred had gone her parents hadn't stopped! Mildred sulked for an entire day until Ms. Rapscott told her, "Look on the bright side, Mildred. Even if it didn't have a letter inside, at least your parents remembered to mail you an envelope. It's more than *I* got."

Mildred came out of her funk long enough to secretly feel happy when Fay was called to the phone and heard a strange voice say: "Press one for English."

Fay pressed one.

The voice said, Press one if you are a boy. Press two if you are a girl."

Fay pressed two.

The voice said, "At the sound of the beep please state your name . . ." BEEEEEEP.

"Fay," said Fay.

"Press one if it is your birthday. Press two if you are away at camp. Press three if you are away at school."

Fay pressed three.

"Hello, Fay—we hope you are having fun at—school. Don't forget to brush your teeth and be a good—girl. Have a nice day. Good-bye." What Fay didn't know was that her parents hadn't slacked off a bit either. In fact they had started taking in foreign exchange students for the summer whose names all started with the letter *Z*. "Oh, phooey!" Fay griped.

"HA!" Ms. Rapscott laughed. "At least *you* got a recorded phone call—I never even got *that*."

"You didn't?" Fay said amazed.

"No, I did not, and as you can see I am none the worse for wear." Ms. Rapscott pursed her lips. "Now pull up your socks and get on with it, Fay."

Fay took the teacher's advice and pulled up her socks, literally, because they always seemed to be in puddles around her ankles. But she had to admit she felt a certain satisfaction when Annabelle's parents sent her a pair of orthotics with a used energy gel wrapper stuck to the bottom of one and an extra-large cap that had BAD HAIR DAY written across the front.

Annabelle's parents had just gotten into the *Guinness Book of World Records* by hopping up Pikes Peak backward on one foot and then down on the other foot. Annabelle stewed, even though she knew in her heart it wasn't that her parents didn't care about her, it was just that they had a lot to do. Even so, it did put a smile on Annabelle's face when Dahlia Thistle got a gift basket with a prepaid gas gift card, some detergent, fabric softener, and a dozen K-Cups with the message: "Have fun at college!" It had come from the lost girl's grandmother's niece Denise's mother, Ruth, who owned several Laundromats, raised llamas, grew heirloom tomatoes, and was probably the busiest in the entire Thistle family.

Ms. Rapscott and Lewis and Clark shook their heads sadly, but really none of the girls felt sorry for one another—not even Dahlia Thistle—which is how it is when you're a daughter of busy parents and you're too busy feeling sorry for yourself.

Once Morning Meeting was over the day's lessons began. You might be thinking that life at Great Rapscott was all flying around in the sky and eating birthday cake, but in fact it was extremely demanding.

"Take notes, girls, for you will be tested and are required to memorize and recite all that you learn each day." Then Clark wrote everything down on the chalkboard.

"The Basics!" Ms. Rapscott said early in the week.

Clark wrote in big letters:

THE BASICS:
1. When to say "please" and "thank you"
2. Sneezing etiquette
3. How to cross the street without getting squashed

During the first week the girls learned things that daughters of busy parents must remember to *never* do.

1. Never drink water from a pond
2. Never stare at the sun
3. Never tease an alligator
4. Never wear plaids with stripes
5. Never take the family car out for a spin

They also learned things that daughters of busy parents should *always* do.

1. Always keep a secret
2. Always wash light and dark clothes separately
3. Always rsvp
4. Always refrigerate after opening
5. Always change your underwear daily

Every day Ms. Rapscott ended their morning lessons with the same warning, "The most important thing to remember is to always, always, ALWAYS hide in your box if you are ever chased by a burglar, bee, mean babysitter, or any other manner of people or things that prey on girls of busy parents. Do you understand?"

The girls nodded solemnly, but their heads were always swimming. They never dreamed there could be so much to learn, so many pitfalls and things to look out for; even Bea, who really hadn't started listening until the one about the alligators, was quiet for a change.

After their morning lessons, lunch, the larg-

est meal of the day at Great Rapscott School, was served in the kitchen. By now you might also think that all Ms. Rapscott ever fed the girls was ice cream and birthday cake, but nothing could have been further from the truth. When everyone was asleep Lewis and Clark fished in the sea and either grilled what they caught or made it into stews, soups, or casseroles. Behind the lighthouse, sheltered from the winds in the corner of an outcrop of boulders, was a large garden with all kinds of vegetables: tomatoes, beans, carrots, broccoli, spinach, you name it. There was also an apple tree and blueberry bushes that grew wild beyond the garden.

At noon the girls gathered around a long wooden table to eat, and as Head Girl, Bea was supposed to dish out the food. This alone was a lesson for Bea, who had only recently learned to use a knife and fork.

Every mealtime at Great Rapscott School was used as an opportunity for instruction. Ms. Rapscott's girls were taught how to bake a potato, make a salad, and poach an egg. As soon as they were finished with lunch the girls were required to help with the dishes and cleaning up, chores that none of them had a clue about until they'd come to Great Rapscott School.

They were graded on pot drying (Bea always tried to put them away wet), table washing (Mildred swept crumbs on the floor more times than not), and putting everything away in its proper place (Fay was particularly challenged at that).

Next were afternoon classes which were designed to sharpen the girls' skills on How to Find Your Way. Ms. Rapscott started with the easiest lessons like How to Find a Missing Sock and worked up to the more demanding lessons like How to Choose the Best Sneakers.

One day toward the end of the week, when the rain finally let up and the sky was blue, she had the girls gather outside in the garden for a new lesson. Before them were hundreds of cantaloupes drying in the sun.

"Girls." The teacher stood with her hands clasped as she did just before she was about to say something important. "When you are trying to Find Your Way you need to know what to look for and have patience. It is exactly the same as knowing how to pick out a good cantaloupe!"

Ms. Rapscott ignored the sound of Annabelle who exhaled loudly through her teeth. "STEP ONE!" the teacher exclaimed. "What to Look for in a Good Cantaloupe." She tiptoed into the melon patch so as not to bruise the fruit with her gigantic boots and hemmed and hawed, picking up melons and putting them down. "Patience, girls! Patience!" she called to her class, until finally she plucked one off the stem and handed it to Lewis, who sliced it down the center to reveal a perfectly ripe fruit. "A good cantaloupe is rather like a Rapscott Girl—never mushy, with no blemishes, or insects, or flies. Yes. We should all endeavor to be like a good cantaloupe. A mighty fruit, bold and proud . . . yet subtle. A Rapscott Girl is always subtle, class."

Annabelle's face by now was purple with anger. She exhaled loudly, rolled her eyes, and flipped her hair. "But what if I don't want to be like a cantaloupe, Ms. Rapscott."

"You should," Ms. Rapscott said. "But only a good cantaloupe, Annabelle. There's nothing worse than a bad one—mushy, tasteless. Good taste is a treasured quality that we must all cultivate, girls. Now come along. Let's see you each pick out a good one."

Bea thought just because it was the biggest cantaloupe it would be a good one, but it was mushy inside.

Mildred was worn out just thinking about picking a good cantaloupe. All she wanted to do was take a nap. So she picked out the first one she saw, but it was dry as a bone and tasted like a pumpkin.

Fay picked out a small watermelon.

Annabelle picked out the prettiest cantaloupe, but it was hard as a rock.

All the girls stood glumly in the cantaloupe patch with their bad cantaloupes.

"You've all failed today!" Ms. Rapscott said cheerfully, and even hopped a little with joy, for she thought that failure was a true sign of effort. "Never fear, girls, with practice you'll get it right."

At 5:00 sharp the girls were happy to be done with lessons and have their tea, which was a light meal of sandwiches followed by pie, for Ms. Rapscott knew that even birthday cake could be too much of a good thing. Shortly thereafter they were given some free time in which the teacher advised them to try as hard as they could to do nothing until bedtime. "Remember, girls, many are busy doing nothing, but some can do nothing but be terribly busy." Ms. Rapscott devoted at least four hours a day herself to doing nothing and tried to instill the habit in her girls.

Mildred made a beeline to her bed and closed the curtains to daydream about being on top of the birthday cake and as brave as Bea.

When it wasn't raining Fay had a favorite rock that she leaned against and looked for Dahlia Thistle through her binoculars.

Annabelle was happy to curl up with the books in the classroom and read something beside the *Encyclopedia Britannica*.

They weren't exactly doing nothing, but Bea did the least amount of nothing of them all. She used the time to creep up to the forbidden floor above their dorm, where a hatch door remained frustratingly locked. She was far more success-ful at short sheeting Annabelle's bed, and even managed to put cold noodles in the girl's shoes, for which Bea got into trouble and had to spend three periods of doing nothing writing on the chalkboard *I will not put cold noodles in Anna-belle's shoes* one hundred times.

Lights were out at 9:00. At first Bea, Mildred, Fay, and Annabelle could find no reason to talk to one another, but finally one night Bea whis-pered over to Mildred, "What do you think is up there on the floor above ours?"

"Maybe a ghost?" Mildred said with a shud-der.

"Maybe a monster," Bea said louder, hoping to scare the others.

"Maybe Ms. Rapscott's boyfriend is up there." Annabelle giggled, and all the girls giggled with her for a change.

When it became quiet again Fay said wistfully, "I wonder where Dahlia Thistle is right now."

Everyone's eyes traveled to the little stuffed lamb on the empty bed.

"I hope she's okay," Mildred muttered.

"I'm sure she's not," Annabelle said as she fluffed up her pillow.

Later that night when everyone was asleep, Fay crept over to the lost girl's bed. She stared into the eyes of the stuffed lamb and held her breath because she half expected him to blink. Light streamed in through a window from a moon that was almost full. "Don't worry," she whispered to him, "we'll find her."

Chapter 10
THE SEASKIMMERS

Overnight the temperature changed, and in the morning Ms. Rapscott bustled into the dorm, her hair all a-frizz. The fisherman's sweater was gone. In its place she wore a navy blue bathing suit with a large skirt that came to her knees and her same old heavy-duty boots.

The girls tried not to laugh.

As Ms. Rapscott clomped around, cheerfully opening up all the windows, she asked, "The first step to Finding Your Way is what, class?"

"Getting Lost on Purpose!" they all answered from their beds.

"When we get Lost on Purpose we never bring a what?"

"A map," Mildred moaned, and put the covers over her head.

"Here we go again," Annabelle muttered.

"Is it a full moon and a high tide?" Fay asked eagerly.

"It is indeed!" Ms. Rapscott exclaimed.

The girls could feel that the weather had turned. A balmy salt breeze blew gently through their room.

"In your boxes, each of you will find your regulation Great Rapscott bathing suit." Ms. Rapscott paused at the stairs. "Please wear it to Morning Meeting today."

"B-but I can't swim, Ms. Rapscott." Mildred's heart began to thud in her chest, and she hadn't even gotten out of bed yet.

"Girls of busy parents can *never* swim, Mildred." Ms. Rapscott disappeared down the stairs, and her voice sounded hollow as she called up to them, "Besides we're not going swimming today—we are going skimming."

Skimming? Bea, Fay, and Annabelle confirmed

that none of them could swim or skim either— whatever that was.

At Morning Meeting Lewis and Clark were busier than usual. Lewis was synchronizing his watch by the big clock on the wall, and Clark was putting things into their backpacks. This made Mildred even more nervous. She remembered the last time Lewis synchronized his watch, and it wasn't much later that she was flying through the air wearing a parachute.

Beatrice, Mildred, Fay, and Annabelle lined up in their nautical-looking one-piece navy blue Rapscott bathing suits with the white piping, the school seal emblazoned on their chests.

Ms. Rapscott stood before them in her over-sized bathing suit, but now there was nothing funny about her. "As you all know the conditions are perfect today to find Dahlia Thistle. This will be an opportunity to continue your studies in How to Find Your Way." Ms. Rapscott glanced at the clock that ticked loudly on the wall. "Are we ready? Lewis? Clark?" Both corgis looked more than ready in their life preservers. "At nine o'clock we will begin. Goggles on, class!"

"G-Goggles?" Mildred stammered. "For what? We're inside."

"Life preservers on, girls!" Ms. Rapscott hurried to get hers. The teacher leaned forward with her arms straight out, and Lewis and Clark slipped her bright orange life preserver over her head and pulled it tightly around her waist.

Bea and Fay went about putting on theirs, while Mildred and Annabelle hesitated.

"I don't see why we need a life preserver to learn How to Find Our Way or Dahlia Thistle," Annabelle said sharply.

"Because, Annabelle, you cannot swim, and if you fall into the water you will sink like a stone and drown. Life preservers on, girls! Quickly! Quickly!" Ms. Rapscott was as irresistible as ever to disobey. Against their better judgment, even Mildred and Annabelle soon found themselves doing what they were told and followed behind Ms. Rapscott in their life preservers and goggles.

Outside, the air felt delicious, but the sea was

swollen and waves broke dangerously on the rocks not ten feet from the girls.

"It looks awfully rough today," Mildred said in a small voice.

"I *know*!" Ms. Rapscott answered. "Isn't it thrilling?" She loved it when the surf reared high against the cliffs, its crests white with foam.

The teacher peered once again through her binoculars to search the sky.

"Do you see her?" the girls all asked at once, but a wave suddenly crashed onto the walkway, and they had to leap back to keep from getting soaked.

"Come along, girls." Ms. Rapscott sloshed through the water and motioned for the girls to follow.

"Closer?" Mildred squeaked.

"Closer, girls!" the teacher cried out.

"Closer?" they said as a group.

"Closer, girls!" she repeated.

"If we move any closer we are going to be *in* the water," Annabelle said sarcastically.

"Precisely!" Ms. Rapscott looked through her

binoculars again and announced. "There they are—right on time!"

"Who?" Bea yelled.

"SHHHHH!!!" Ms. Rapscott cupped an ear. "Can you hear them?"

"Hear who?" Bea yelled to be heard over the surf.

"The Seaskimmers are coming—get ready, girls." Lewis and Clark took their places beside the teacher.

Out in the ocean the girls could see five dark round heads bobbing up and down. They came nearer and nearer to the shore. *"ARK! ARK! ARK!"* The air was filled with the sounds of barking.

"They're seals!" Annabelle exclaimed.

"Incorrect, Annabelle! These are Seaskimmers!" Ms. Rapscott said.

Annabelle had never read a thing in the encyclopedia about any Seaskimmers. Then again she'd never read anything about Skysweepers or Bumbershoot Trees either. Annabelle took a deep breath and tightened her life preserver.

The sea boiled with whitecaps, and another wave broke close to the lighthouse and flooded the porch. As the water receded Bea held on to the sturdy Great Rapscott School signpost, Mildred held on to Bea, Fay held on to Mildred, and Annabelle held on to Fay to keep from being swept out to sea.

"Since Bea is Head Girl this week, she can go first," Ms. Rapscott said. By now there were five large shiny black animals swimming in a circle. They looked like seals but jumped and somersaulted out of the water like dolphins.

Bea had liked being Head Girl, but as she eyed the choppy black water that the strange sea animals cavorted in, a chill slithered down her spine. When Clark swooped her up under her arms and plunked her onto the back of one, she tried not to look scared—though it wasn't easy. The Seaskimmer was slippery as a snake. She dug in her knees and held on for dear life.

"ARK! ARK! ARK!" the other Seaskimmers barked playfully. Soon one by one even Mildred

was astride hers. Then Ms. Rapscott and the dogs held their noses and jumped into the ocean. *SPLASH!* They popped up like corks and in moments were seated on the largest Seaskimmer of all. Ms. Rapscott rode in front; Lewis held on to her waist, and Clark held on to Lewis. The three looked like they'd been riding these animals all their lives.

"Say hello to your Seaskimmers, girls!" Ms. Rapscott's leaped gracefully out of the water. "A Rapscott Girl is always friendly."

"H-Hello, Seaskimmer." Mildred clung to hers with her arms around its neck.

"Follow me, girls!" Ms. Rapscott, along with Lewis and Clark, rode away from the lighthouse out into deeper water where it was less rough. They followed along the cliffs of the island; all the while the Seaskimmers barked excitedly, *"ARK! ARK! ARK!"*

"I know these cliffs by heart!" Ms. Rapscott shouted confidently.

They raced across the ocean like this, barely

breaking the surface, for some time. At first Bea, Mildred, Fay, and Annabelle were terrified being out in the middle of the ocean, skimming along on the back of some animal they'd never even heard of.

Bea was the first to get the knack of riding one.

Fay, too, became more comfortable on her Seaskimmer. She was soon riding alongside Bea, expertly sliding up one side of the waves and down the other, confirming Ms. Rapscott's theory that a sparkle in the eye truly is a sign of an adventurous spirit.

Annabelle rode behind Bea and Fay, her mouth wide open, her eyes big behind the goggles, her long black hair whipped in the wind. All matter of horrible scenes crowded her mind: sunburned to a crisp from the UV rays, stung by jellyfish, and most grisly—toppling off and being gobbled up by sharks. Worry took up every nook and cranny in her brain, which is how it is when you've been reading the *Encyclopedia Britannica* your whole life.

Mildred's Seaskimmer was the fattest and the slowest, which she was thankful for. She leaned over what should have been his shoulders, if he'd had any, and wrapped her arms around his neck in a death grip. After the first minute aboard she gave up trying to hold on with her knees, and her legs streamed out behind her.

Meanwhile the sun sparkled off the water that was as warm as a bathtub. People on the shore waved, totally unconcerned by the sight of the girls. Bea and Fay waved back, but Annabelle and Mildred just grimaced, too afraid to free a hand to wave.

"ARK! ARK! ARK!" the Seaskimmers barked with delight.

They slowed now for a time and glided past small towns, busy harbors, and sailboats. Annabelle kept her eyes on her Seaskimmer and her knees bunched up for fear of fish nibbling her toes. Mildred lay on top of hers, catching her breath, and then, feeling it safe, she risked getting up on one elbow. Through a curtain of wet and tangled hair, she could see children playing on the beaches and paddling in the waves, but none of them was Dahlia Thistle.

Fay watched the land for the lost girl, too, but there was absolutely no sign of her.

"I know these beaches like the back of my hand!" Ms. Rapscott called to the girls. Behind them the lighthouse blinked but was becoming farther and farther away.

Atop their Seaskimmers they curved around the island, and Great Rapscott vanished from sight. There were no people here. The cliffs were lower and the trees were taller. The farther they traveled, the higher and more lush the vegetation became.

"I know this part of the island by heart!" Ms. Rapscott shouted out.

"Where are we?" Bea yelled.

"And where's Dahlia Thistle?" Fay called. But both girls' words were drowned out by the seagulls that careered overhead, screaming and dipping into the water for fish.

They slowed even more now, and Annabelle ventured to look up. The island seemed as big as the world. Formations of smooth rounded rocks cropped out here and there. They were heading inland.

Their Seaskimmers surfed the white frothy waves that bubbled to the shore and, in moments, they all washed up onto a beach covered with pink sand.

"Say 'thank you,' class," Ms. Rapscott said, and she and Lewis and Clark shook their Seaskimmer's flipper and made little bows.

The girls did the same with each of theirs.

"ARK! ARK!" The enormous sea creatures leaped back through the waves. When they got to the open water, they turned and barked their good-byes and then raced off, skimming over the water and out of sight.

Chapter 11

LOOKING FOR DAHLIA THISTLE

The group stood on the pink sand, their suits drying in the sun. Bea, Mildred, Fay, and Annabelle snapped off their goggles, and all around them was a tropical paradise. Palm trees swayed in the breeze, and rhododendron grew high in the forest at the end of the beach. Green parrots with silver bellies swooped overhead and roosted in giant avocado trees. Yellow fish darted about in the crystal clear turquoise water. Bright pink, purple, and orange flowers bloomed in a riot of color everywhere.

"Boots and binoculars out, girls!" Ms. Rapscott ordered. Soon they were an odd sight to see, wearing bathing suits, with boots, looking through their binoculars. Ms. Rapscott peered through hers. "Question number one! Do you know where Dahlia Thistle is?"

"NO!" the girls answered as a group.

"Question number two!" Ms. Rapscott asked, "Which way should we go to find Dahlia Thistle?"

The girls looked again through their binoculars. In one direction weeds sprouted through the cracks of a strip of crumbling pavement with a crooked signpost stuck in the sand that said LESS TRAVELED ROAD. Crossing it was a newly paved road with a lovely white stripe smack down the middle of it, a sidewalk, lampposts, curbs, and a sturdy sign that read: WELL TRAVELED ROAD. It was even filled with shiny cars that honked as they cruised by with happy people inside them.

"I think we should take this road!" Annabelle pointed to Well Traveled Road and all the others, except for Bea (who refused to agree with Annabelle on anything), thought it looked like a very good road to them, too.

Ms. Rapscott bristled at the suggestion, and Lewis and Clark poked their noses in the air and shook their heads from side to side.

"But why not?" Annabelle wanted to know.

"Because you will see many more interesting things on Less Traveled Road," Ms. Rapscott replied. "Remember, class, curiosity is always favorable to convenience." Clark clicked his pen and wrote: *Curiosity is always favorable to convenience*, on his clipboard under the heading, "Remark of the Day," for Ms. Rapscott to use at Morning Meeting.

"Come along, Beatrice, you are Head Girl!" Ms. Rapscott called over her shoulder. She and Lewis and Clark started down Less Traveled Road.

Bea caught up to the teacher while the others followed, but they turned and looked longingly at Well Traveled Road. Two people on bicycles pedaled by, as if to say, "Come this way!"

Less Traveled Road went straight into the forest that loomed dark and mysterious. As soon as they entered, the road became nothing more than a narrow path. Even more unsettling, they couldn't miss a bright orange life preserver lying under a bushy fern. Lewis examined it, and Clark made a notation.

"Dahlia Thistle's life preserver!" Ms. Rapscott exclaimed.

It was covered with sand and leaves. The group stared at it solemnly, each wondering what fate had befallen the missing girl.

"Don't worry, girls. Dahlia Thistle obviously discarded it." Ms. Rapscott assured them. "When Finding Your Way it is always wise to lighten your load!"

Farther down the path Lewis and Clark found something else.

"Dahlia Thistle's shoes that she obviously discarded as well." Ms. Rapscott held them upside down, and sand poured out of them. "Remember, class, when Finding Your Way, always wear boots." Clark made another notation.

A sense of doom came over the girls.

The trees closed in around them. Long strands of moss grew thickly and hung off branches like a haunted fairy-tale wood. The green and silver birds soared and circled, but it was eerily quiet. Bea hurried forward, anxious to keep her position as leader the entire way, not even stopping to eat her crackers and cheese or drink from the huge tropical leaves of passionflowers that held cups of sweet nectar.

Fay turned around to look for Annabelle and Mildred, but they lagged far behind and were nowhere to be seen. She jogged up beside Bea. "Don't you think we should slow down for the others?"

"I'm Head Girl." Bea dodged rocks and roots with nimble feet. She did not want to lose her position on top of the birthday cake. "I'm not waiting for anybody!"

Fay had the uneasy feeling that maybe she *should* wait for Mildred. On the other hand, she didn't want to get lost like Dahlia Thistle, so she hurried to keep up with Bea.

Annabelle exhaled loudly through her teeth. She felt it her duty, as the only responsible person in the group, to stay back to look after Mil-

dred, which is how it is when you are Old for Your Age. But Mildred stopped often. "Look at that!" At her feet was a silver feather that sparkled in a beam of sun, shining on the path. She picked it up to keep as a souvenir.

Annabelle yelled impatiently, "Come on!"

Around the bend Mildred stopped again and pointed.

"Wild orchids, big deal," Annabelle yawned. She'd read all about them in the encyclopedia a thousand times. "Can't you go any faster, Mildred?"

But Mildred never knew the world outside her bedroom could be so dazzling, and she stopped again to look at tall slender trees that grew hundreds of feet high.

"Giant bamboo." Annabelle pulled Mildred's hand to get going again.

They passed a gray, smooth-barked tree, and Mildred whistled at the size of its trunk—too big even if all four Rapscott girls held hands and tried to get their arms around it.

"Banyan tree." Annabelle rolled her eyes.

"Come *on*, Mildred—we're going to get left behind!"

But suddenly Mildred noticed something *really* interesting, just like Ms. Rapscott said they would. "Look!" Above, an enormous bright green bird with a vest of silver feathers looked down from his nest that was as big as her bedroom back home. Above it hung a parachute as a roof, which kept it cozy and dry. "Hello up there!" Mildred called to the bird. "Have you seen Dahlia Thistle?"

The bird's round black eyes grew large. A moment later his wings fanned out and he fluttered down to them onto Less Traveled Road. In his beak was an envelope, and Mildred immediately recognized it as one of the same note cards that she had in her own backpack! He dropped it in Mildred's hands and flew back to his tree.

Annabelle huffed. She was annoyed that she hadn't seen the nest first. "Come on!" Before Mildred could read the note, Annabelle yanked the girl by the arm, pulling her down the trail.

When Ms. Rapscott finally appeared, Mildred

ran straight to the teacher with the note, and she read aloud what Dahlia Thistle had written:

Dear Ms. Rapscott,

I know you are probably very busy with your school and all and probably won't find this note but in case you do I was here. The nest was nice, though the bird ate a lot of worms and I don't like them, but I'm little and don't eat much so I had plenty of crackers and cheese. Thanks! I am on my way to you and hope I find your school someday.

Your student,
Dahlia Thistle

p.s. Also, tell my lamb I am okay. I don't want him to worry.

"Splendid note. Excellent punctuation, spelling, penmanship, A + . . . and spoken like a true Rapscott Girl!" the teacher said proudly, and then turned to Lewis and Clark. "She may be Known for Being a Late Bloomer, but Dahlia Thistle is Wise for Her Age."

A + ? Annabelle didn't think that Dahlia Thistle's note was so great. "If Dahlia Thistle is all that wise, why is she lost?" Annabelle's glasses fogged up from her bad temper, and the hair stuck to her forehead in sweaty clumps. It had been an annoying afternoon. "We're never going to find her—she's as lost as Amelia Earhart."

"Who's Amelia Earhart?" Mildred asked.

"She was the first woman to fly a plane solo across the Atlantic Ocean," Annabelle said knowingly. She had read all about her in the *Encyclopedia Britannica.*

Ms. Rapscott added, "Amelia Earhart had pluck, enthusiasm, spirit of adventure, brilliance, and self-reliance."

"And she was never found," Annabelle said smugly, "just like Dahlia Thistle."

Ms. Rapscott looked straight ahead as she walked but would not say another word. The path rounded a corner. Less Traveled Road was now quite wide here, and sitting in the middle of it was a very old, small aircraft. Lewis and Clark were already at the controls.

"What a coincidence!" Ms. Rapscott glanced at Annabelle. "Here we were just talking about Amelia Earhart, and there is her very airplane. You do see the most interesting things on Less Traveled Road!"

Annabelle's mouth gaped open. The plane looked exactly like the one she had seen in pictures of Amelia Earhart's that had completely vanished!

"Come along, class." Ms. Rapscott climbed aboard, and the girls scrambled in after her. Bea, Mildred, Fay, and Annabelle sat behind Ms. Rapscott while Lewis and Clark started the engine, and soon they were taxiing down Less Traveled Road.

"Is this really Amelia Earhart's plane?" Annabelle shouted.

But Ms. Rapscott seemed not to hear.

That night, while the girls were snug in their familiar dorm room, their teacher appeared once again. She was back in her fisherman's sweater, mud brown pants, and boots. She bustled round the room, closing all the windows. The rain pattered softly at first, but soon they could hear it thrumming against the lighthouse. The wind rattled the windows and the lights flickered. It was cold again. Their tropical adventure seemed like a dream now, as if none of the things that day had ever happened.

Had they really ridden the Seaskimmers and flown home in Amelia Earhart's plane?

Mildred reached into her backpack and there at the bottom of it was the silver feather. She held it in her hand and stared at it till she fell asleep.

Chapter 12

HOW TO TURN BAD LUCK INTO GOOD LUCK

It was the beginning of their second week at Great Rapscott School, and the girls woke up again to a dark, dreary day. They gathered in the round classroom for Morning Meeting. On the chalkboard once more was the drawing of the birthday cake with the five pieces of paper that they knew covered each of their names.

Bea was confident that she would remain on top of the birthday cake this week. Hadn't she led the entire way yesterday, right out in front, always first? Bea grinned to herself. It was great to be Head Girl, and now she just wished she'd gone even faster.

Mildred hated the stupid birthday cake. She sat in her chair anxiously twirling her hair around a finger.

Ms. Rapscott nodded to Clark that it was time to begin. With a flick of her wrist, she pulled the first piece of paper off the bottom of the cake to reveal a name.

"Beatrice!" Ms. Rapscott said. The color drained from Beatrice's stricken face.

Bea yelled, "This isn't fair!" She stuck out her bottom lip, "I'm the fastest one here— I'm always first!"

"Beatrice, you showed the most promise last week, but this week you scurried ahead and were busy doing nothing. You never considered Mildred, the slowest member of your class. You should be a role model, Beatrice—you weren't, and now you're at the bottom of the birthday cake!" Ms. Rapscott said, quite pleased.

Bea gave the teacher a glowering look.

"Why so glum, Beatrice?" Ms. Rapscott said,

surprised. "It's wonderful to be at the bottom—you have nowhere to go but up!"

Bea pressed her lips together. She was not happy. Ms. Rapscott nodded again at Clark and swiped off the next piece of paper. "Annabelle!"

"Again?" Annabelle cried incredulously. "But I stayed with Mildred the entire time!"

"Annabelle, you continue to underwhelm me. Yes, you stayed with Mildred, but you were not cheerful about it. A Rapscott Girl helps others with a smile." Ms. Rapscott smiled just to demonstrate her point.

Annabelle angrily flipped her hair and stole a look at Bea, who made a face at her, so Annabelle made a face back.

"Next up the cake is . . ." Ms. Rapscott showed them the next name.

"Fay! You did *think* about waiting for Mildred . . . but you let Bea's behavior influence you." The teacher gave the girl a stern look. Fay had been satisfied to be in the middle, but now her smile faded. "A Rapscott Girl is never influenced by others, Fay."

Clark pointed to the next paper, and Ms. Rapscott pulled it off.

"Dahlia Thistle!" she announced. "Dahlia wrote a great note and has handled herself like a Rapscott Girl should. I'd put her at the top of the cake, but she's not here to be Head Girl. I hope we find her someday."

The girls were hardly listening—they couldn't believe that Mildred was at the top of the cake!

"Mildred, you are at the top of the birthday cake this week because you performed like a true Rapscott Girl—even though you were last, you are now first!"

Mildred's cheeks got red and she looked down at her hands, embarrassed, but she couldn't stop smiling.

"You took time to notice what was around you and enjoyed your journey down Less Traveled Road and because of that you spotted the nest with Dahlia Thistle's note. Outstanding job!" Ms. Rapscott looked proudly at the girl.

Lewis and Clark stepped forward to shake Mildred's hand.

"Now Mildred will be Head Girl this week!" Ms. Rapscott exclaimed and then, with a note of warning in her voice, added, "Let's see if you can stay there."

The second week at Great Rapscott was even busier than the first as the girls advanced on to more difficult material like: The Uses of Dental Floss and ChapStick, the Difference Between Tall Kitchen Garbage Bags versus Heavy Duty Trash Bags, and How to Grow a Carrot. As usual they continued their studies in How to Find Your Way.

One day at the end of the week a tornado had just twirled by and now a hurricane blew waves almost as tall as the lighthouse. Ms. Rapscott stood before them in the classroom and said, "It's a good day for Bad Luck, girls!" Just then the door opened with a *BANG!* Rain and wind burst into the classroom and everyone watched a soaking wet Lewis and Clark slosh inside with a large dripping orange ladder. Then the corgis opened it up and set it in the middle of the room.

Ms. Rapscott continued, "In order to Find Your Way, class, you need to have a lot of Good

Luck. Unfortunately, daughters of busy parents typically have a lot of *Bad* Luck." Here the teacher looked into the eyes of each girl as if she could see just how much bad luck they each had. Then she asked, "Question number one. How Do You Turn Bad Luck into Good Luck?"

Annabelle raised her hand right away, "You get a rabbit's foot. I read all about it once."

"Wrong!" Ms. Rapscott exclaimed. "It wasn't very lucky for the rabbit, and it won't be lucky for you either."

Annabelle folded her arms and scowled.

"To begin with, you must first know What Gives You Bad Luck." Ms. Rapscott stood by the chalkboard, "Bad Luck!" she declared, and Clark wrote down her list.

BAD LUCK:
1. Never break a mirror
2. Never put shoes on a bed
3. Never cross paths with a black cat
4. Never pick up a dropped penny if it's tails up
5. Never walk under a ladder

"Mildred, since you are Head Girl this week, I would like you to walk under that ladder." Ms. Rapscott pointed to the one the corgis had just brought inside.

"But it's Bad Luck, Ms. Rapscott. I'm afraid!" Mildred's eyes became glassy with tears.

"It is also extremely Bad Luck, Mildred, to cry when you get Bad Luck."

"It is?" Mildred had stopped crying, but she wouldn't budge from her seat.

"Nevermind, *I* will walk under the ladder, girls!" The teacher squared her shoulders, threw her back head, and marched off.

"DON'T!" Bea shouted. "Something bad will happen—you just said so!"

"Of course something *bad* will happen, Beatrice. What would be the sense of walking under a ladder otherwise?" the teacher replied.

All the girls gasped as she strode under it as if it were the most fun—which it was—for there was nothing Ms. Rapscott loved better than to have Bad Luck just so that she could turn it into Good Luck.

The girls all held their breath and watched the teacher as if she might explode. But she didn't, and they were relieved that by the time she was back at the chalkboard nothing bad had happened.

She started to speak, "Now class—*ACHOO*—*ACHOO! ACH-OO! AH-AH-AH-AHCHOOOOOOOOOO!!!!!*" Ms. Rapscott sneezed so hard that a stack of papers on her desk flew into the air, up to the ceiling, and fluttered down to the floor.

"HA!" She blew her nose and shook her head, "Good news, girls! I've got a cold. *ACH-OO!* I am officially having—*ACHOO!*—Bad Luck. I must go to bed immediately."

The girls watched in bewilderment as the teacher turned on her heels and disappeared up the spiral stairs. Then they ran after her to see what would happen next.

Of course, up until then, they'd never been allowed to go higher in the lighthouse than their own floor. Except for Bea, none of them had even tried. Now the fifth floor was finally unlocked, and the girls could tell they were walking into

Ms. Rapscott's room. Already, she was covered up with a heavy wool blanket, which had a black, red, yellow, and green stripe, in a bed that looked like it had once been a large rowboat. Across from her were Lewis's and Clark's two bunks that came out from the wall and were held in place with heavy ropes like you'd see coiled on the deck of a ship. Their beds were all made up with a pillow each and the same striped blankets. It was a cozy room with hundreds of books, and in an alcove was a little woodstove.

"Girls." Ms. Rapscott's nose had already become so stuffy she could barely speak. "Ben you are trying to Find Your Bay you bill need a' know Howda' Turn Bad Luck inda' Good. *ACHOO!*" The girls stood around the bed with their notebooks and pencils ready.

"STEB ONE! Always knock on wood ben your temberture is normbal." Lewis handed her a thermometer, and she popped it in her mouth.

Now, everyone, knows that anything above 98.6 means that you have a fever, but none of these girls had ever heard of such a thing—except for Annabelle, who'd read all about it. There was a little beep, and Ms. Rapscott handed the thermometer to Bea, who looked at it, shrugged, and handed it to Mildred, who had no idea, either, what the numbers meant. She handed it to Fay, who was completely flummoxed, so she handed it to Annabelle, who said astutely, "Ninety-eight point six! Which is a normal temperature for a human being."

"You didn't knock on wood, BAD LUCK!" Ms. Rapscott moaned.

All the girls gathered anxiously around the teacher, only to see the numbers on the thermometer suddenly change for the worse.

"One hundred and four degrees?" Annabelle cried with dismay. "You have a very high fever!"

"I don' feel so good." Ms. Rapscott lay back on the pillows and closed her eyes. The girls stared at her, afraid of what would happen next. She opened one eye. "Perhabs I should take my temberture again." In her mouth went the thermometer. The girls waited tensely for the little beep. Then she handed it to Fay to read.

Fay's face broke into a grin, "Ninety-eight point six—knock on wood!"

"Good Luck! I feel buch bedder!" Ms. Rapscott said, but her nose was still bright red. "Steb two! It's always lucky, girls, to drink a *good* cub of four-leaf-clober tea ben you have a bad cold." She blew her nose and made a honking noise. The girls giggled, and she gave them a wan look. "How do you make four-leaf-clober tea? Adybody?"

None of the girls, not even Annabelle, raised their hands, because they didn't know how to make *any* kind of tea really.

Ms. Rapscott got out of her bed and went over to the woodstove where a kettle sat steaming on the top. She poured water from it into a mug from a shelf nearby. She squeezed part of a lemon and then dipped a spoon into a jar of honey and mixed a large amount into her cup, "Be liberal wib 'da hodey, girls," she instructed over her shoulder. Next she pulled a tin canister off the same shelf and picked through it till she found the biggest four-leaf clover and proceeded to hold it by the stem and dunk it in the tea several times.

"AH-AH-ACHOO!" she sneezed. Next she took a big gulp of the tea. "Perfect!" she said. "I am feeling buch, *buch* bedder!" Lewis and Clark made their own cups of tea with the same process and then clinked their mugs together.

"A good cub of four-leaf-clober tea is rather like a Rabscott Girl—strong but neber bidder." She finished off the rest of her tea and went to make some more. Her nose was already less red and stuffed up. "Yes, class, we must all strive to be like a good cup of four-leaf-clover tea."

Annabelle was huffing and exhaling loudly more than ever and finally erupted, "What if I don't want to be like a cup of tea?"

"As I recall, you did not want to be like an asparagus or a cantaloupe either." Ms. Rapscott gave Clark a knowing look, and he wrote something down in his notes. Ignoring Annabelle, Ms. Rapscott remarked, "Furthermore, girls, you want to be like a *good* cup of tea. For a *bad* cup is weak, pale, and tepid. A Rapscott Girl is never tepid," she said gravely, and jumped back under the covers.

Pretty soon they were all sitting on the teacher's bed, which was like a boat, learning how to play checkers, which she said was also a way to turn Bad Luck into Good when you have a cold.

A while later, as the waves lashed and shook the lighthouse, the lights flickered off, and birthday candles were lit so they could see. Annabelle had just won the last three rounds of checkers when Mildred noticed that Ms. Rapscott hadn't even sneezed or coughed for quite some time.

"Are you all better?" she asked.

"I *am*, Mildred, that was *very* considerate of you to ask." The teacher hopped out of bed quite well. "A Rapscott Girl is always considerate, class!"

Annabelle scrunched up her face, and her glasses fell down to the tip of her nose. "I don't see how this turns Bad Luck into Good." But Bea, Mildred, and Fay did understand the lesson, because that afternoon Ms. Rapscott had had an awful cold and now it was gone—everything she had told them about luck had been true!

"And if you want something good to happen,

try crossing your fingers, girls." Ms. Rapscott demonstrated with two of her own, and just before she disappeared down the spiral staircase the lights came back on.

That night Bea, Mildred, Fay, and Annabelle stayed up late talking. The conversation turned to Dahlia Thistle, who obviously wasn't having any Good Luck at all. Had she broken a mirror? Picked up the wrong side of a penny? Had she crossed paths with a black cat or walked under a ladder? The girls' attention was drawn to the empty yellow bed where the woolly lamb was propped forlornly against the pillow.

"Have you noticed," Fay said in low voice, "that his eyes follow you wherever you go?"

None of the others had, but now that she mentioned it they could see it.

"And look how sad he is." Fay seemed to have a sixth sense about how someone else was feeling.

It was true. Bea and Mildred said, "He looks like he just lost his best friend."

"He did," Annabelle said. Then she gave them

a good dose of grown-up reality. "Dahlia Thistle is probably mashed under a rock by now."

"Oh, I hope not!" Fay said, and crossed her fingers under her purple quilt.

Here Annabelle repeated a phrase she had heard often from adults, "Well, I think we should expect the worst."

"Well *I* think we should go out and look for her ourselves!" Bea sat in her blue bed in her Rapscott underwear, her short dark hair stuck out belligerently all over her head, and her mouth was set in a determined straight line. Even though Bea was no longer Head Girl, she was pluckier than ever. She hated being at the bottom of the birthday cake and was ready to take matters into her own hands and rescue Dahlia Thistle. If that didn't put her back on top, nothing would. But the others weren't so sure.

Mildred hugged her knees in her green bed and kept quiet, lest the others think she was a coward, which she fully admitted to herself she was.

"I'm with you, Bea!" Fay's teeth still stuck out

like a rabbit's, but the sparkle in her eyes was becoming more noticeable by the day. She couldn't stop thinking about Dahlia Thistle out there all alone.

Annabelle, who considered herself the voice of reason for the group, disagreed. "What if we become just as lost as she is?" She pushed her chin out in the direction of the empty yellow bed.

Bea purposely ignored Annabelle's remark. Mildred shuddered thinking about becoming just as lost as Dahlia, and Fay had made up her mind to bring the stuffed lamb with her when they went in search of the lost girl.

Chapter 13

NOT LOOKING FOR DAHLIA THISTLE

The next morning when Bea woke up she was more determined than ever to go find Dahlia Thistle. "We just have to go get her ourselves."

Annabelle grumbled wearily from her pink bed.

Mildred threw back the curtains of her green bed. "But how do we find her ourselves?" As Head Girl she tried to keep the fear out of her voice, but she was sure it was a bad idea and had no intention of going any farther than five feet past the lighthouse without Ms. Rapscott or Lewis and Clark.

"I know," Fay said excitedly as they all entered the bathroom. "We can tie our bedsheets together, throw them out the window, and climb down them like a rope tonight. Then we can go off and find Dahlia Thistle ourselves!"

Bea's head jerked up from her sink. "What a great idea," she said with a mouth full of tooth-paste, and could already see herself back on top of the cake for sure.

"It'll be so much fun!" Fay spun in a circle. She couldn't wait to see the look on Dahlia This-tle's face when she gave her back her lamb.

"It's a perfectly *awful* idea." Annabelle dried her face with a pink towel. It was lucky for them she was there, Annabelle thought. She was the only one of the bunch with a grain of common sense. If only Ms. Rapscott could see that! Anna-belle repeated, "It'll be a disaster."

"No it won't." Bea stood in her underwear and glared at Annabelle.

"First of all, you'll fall and get squashed on the ground just climbing down bedsheets tied to-gether by her." Annabelle pointed a thumb over her shoulder at Fay. In a brilliant flash of insight,

Annabelle suddenly saw a way to get off the bottom of the birthday cake and said, "Second of all . . . I'll tell."

"But I don't want to go off on our own tonight to go find Dahlia Thistle!" Mildred yelled. All this talk of falling and getting squashed on the ground was giving Mildred a stomachache.

"Well then, don't come!" Bea stomped angrily out of the bathroom, but she immediately felt badly for yelling at Mildred. It wasn't her she was mad at; it was Annabelle. She liked Mildred—she just thought she made a crummy Head Girl.

At Morning Meeting Ms. Rapscott stood before the girls with her hands clasped and an expectant look on her face—like something really good was about to happen—though this was nothing that the girls could be too hopeful about: Good things to Ms. Rapscott were usually exceedingly unpleasant for the rest of them. After all, she enjoyed torrential rain and huge waves. She even enjoyed having Bad Luck.

Mildred was asked to write down the Remark of the Day, which was equally puzzling:

Sometimes when you stop looking, you find things where you least expect them.

"Good news, class!" Ms. Rapscott reached for something on her desk that looked like a paper plane. "We've had word from Dahlia Thistle!" There was applause and loud YAYs! from the girls. The teacher's eyes lit up as she unfolded and then read the note.

Dear Ms. Rapscott,

I followed the light like you said to the top of a mountain in the Alps, but you are not here. I'm too little to climb down alone, but I am fine except that I miss my lamb.

Your student,
Dahlia Thistle

Dahlia Thistle was fine? How was it possible for such a small girl to be on top of a mountain, alone, and fine? The merry mood instantly evaporated.

But Ms. Rapscott seemed unconcerned, jolly in fact, which was really no surprise since being alone on top of a mountain was probably one of her favorite places to be. "Let's write back, shall we?" She dictated to Clark:

Dear Dahlia,

Just as I suspected, there is more to you than being a Late Bloomer. You are right: It would be foolish of you to attempt to climb down alone—you are Wise Beyond Your Years not to try.
I hope we find you someday soon.

Sincerely,
Ms. Rapscott and your classmates

"Now, quickly, everyone sign it." When they had, Ms. Rapscott folded the note into a paper plane and strode over to the window to launch it.

The big clock ticked loudly on the wall behind her. Lewis checked it against his watch. Mildred

noticed and held her breath. She remembered that the last two times he did that she had ended up flying through the air wearing a parachute and skimming along the ocean on top of some strange sea creature. What would be next?

Ms. Rapscott took a deep breath through her large nose and closed her eyes, as if she were thinking very hard. Then she opened them and said with the utmost of confidence, "After giving this careful consideration, class, I have finally decided the reason you have not found Dahlia Thistle by now is that You Are Trying Too Hard."

She gave a nod to Lewis and Clark, and they trotted out of the room. While she waited for the corgis to return, the teacher paced in front of the class thoughtfully. She suddenly stopped and said, "To find Dahlia Thistle we must Look Without Looking."

Annabelle started to sputter as she usually did at such times, but before she could exhale loudly through her teeth, Lewis and Clark appeared, carrying an enormous pile of backpacks, official Rapscott down jackets and pants, snow boots, wool hats, and scarves. The teacher plucked a quilted jacket out of the bunch and tried it on. "Fits perfectly!" she said, pleased, and pulled on a matching pair of navy blue pants right over her old brown ones.

"Are we going off to find Dahlia Thistle?" Fay said hopefully.

Ms. Rapscott secured her hat firmly on her head, "No, Fay, we are going off to *not* find Dahlia Thistle."

"*Not* find her?" Annabelle said indignantly. Lewis and Clark offered her a down jacket and pants that were in the school colors.

"We must Look Without Looking!" Ms. Rapscott sailed around to the back of the classroom and threw open the door. "Boots on, girls!" The group scurried to get their snow boots onto their feet.

Lewis checked his watch. It was 9:00 sharp.

Z-Z-Z-Z-Z-I-I-I-I-P! Clark zipped Annabelle's jacket up to her chin.

"Come along, class," Ms. Rapscott called to them.

They followed their teacher out of the lighthouse bundled up for the Alps. For once the weather was sunny and warm. It was a perfect day—unless you were one of Ms. Rapscott's girls who were roasting inside their arctic outfits.

Everyone was on edge. Bea listened for Skysweeper Winds.

Mildred scanned the ocean for Seaskimmers.

Fay thought that Amelia Earhart's plane might take them to the Alps.

Annabelle thought it was all a lot of nonsense.

Ms. Rapscott stood underneath the Great Rapscott School signpost, which creaked in the soft breeze. "We're off to Not Find Dahlia Thistle!" Ms. Rapscott looked through her binoculars intently. "It's high time we didn't find her—don't you think?"

The wool hat came down over Mildred's forehead, the heavy jacket came up to her chin, and the scarf covered her mouth. All you could see of her face were her eyes and her nose. As Head Girl she thought she should ask, so she mumbled through layers of down and wool, "But where are the Alps?"

"Switzerland," Annabelle said.

"Wrong!" Ms. Rapscott strode away. The girls reluctantly followed.

Mildred hesitated, "But what if we get lost again, Ms. Rapscott?"

Ms. Rapscott looked up at the lighthouse and its beacon blinked reassuringly. "Follow the light!" she called to them. "Always remember to follow the light, girls!"

They grumbled all the way down the road that ran alongside the cliff. Mildred walked along at her own pokey pace, which the others were glad of, for a change. They were in no hurry to start this adventure.

The road turned and all they could see was the very top of the lighthouse. Coming toward them was a lady carrying a parasol, wearing a hat with a sunflower, walking her cat. She looked them up and down. "Going to buy ice cream, eh?"

Mildred spoke first, which she thought her duty as Head Girl. "No, we're Not Looking for Dahlia Thistle in the Alps. Is it far?"

"It's at the end of town." The lady pursed her

lips in disapproval. "But I hear there's a storm coming!"

Storm? It was the most beautiful day Mildred had ever seen. In fact she wished it would get colder—she was sweltering inside her jacket and down pants.

They continued on. Bea marched along the road full of pluck, pretending she was Head Girl once again. Mildred followed full of trepidation. Fay patted the large pocket on her coat where she had Dahlia's lamb safely stowed. Annabelle kept her wits about her.

When they reached the town, they passed an old man who hobbled by. "Not a very good day for buying ice cream, you know," he muttered.

"We're *not* buying ice cream." Annabelle shook her head and realized it wasn't just Ms. Rapscott. Everyone in the entire town was odd.

Mildred added politely, like she thought a Rapscott Girl should, "We're *Not* Looking for Dahlia Thistle."

"Oh well, I hope you don't find her," he called to them.

Bea caught Mildred's eye and grinned. She walked next to the red-haired girl, hoping there were no hard feelings. When Mildred grinned back, Bea was relieved.

The teacher kept up a brisk pace, and the girls followed her through the town, past the grocery store, the bakery, the museum, the movie theater, and the candy store. Finally they passed a lunch-eonette and headed out of town, but they saw no sign of the Alps.

Mildred was hot. She pushed her hat off her forehead, and her jacket was unzipped and hang-ing off her shoulders. She stopped and looked all around.

Bea craned her neck to see. Ms. Rapscott and Lewis and Clark had disappeared around a curve in the road. The land as far as the eye could see was as flat as a pancake, and each girl thought to herself that the likelihood of the Alps being anything less than days and days away was zero to none. But when they turned the corner, there before them was the strangest building.

"Wow!" said Annabelle. Even she was impressed.

A dome-shaped silver structure with huge glass windows glittered blue and green in the sun. There was an enormous sign arched over the doors, surrounded by twinkly blue lights in capital letters that said: THE ALPS.

Chapter 14
THE ALPS

The roof swirled around three times, becoming smaller with each turn, and curled to a sharp point at the very top.

"It looks like a giant ice-cream cone," Fay said in a hushed voice.

The glass doors silently swished open all on their own. As they stepped inside Bea, Mildred, Fay, and Annabelle were immediately glad for their arctic clothing. It was freezing in the cavernous building. The girls' images were reflected in the pale ice-green marble floor they stood on. Gray clouds floated toward what seemed impossibly far away to be a ceiling.

Beams of blue, green, yellow, and pink undulated above their heads. "It's the Aurora Borealis!"

Annabelle's breath frosted the air.

"The what?" Bea wrinkled her nose and craned her neck to see.

"The Northern Lights—you know like up at the North Pole," Annabelle said. The effect was so spellbinding that Bea and Annabelle completely forgot for a moment how much they disliked each other.

Glass and stainless-steel counters lined the circumference of the store where hundreds of tubs of different flavored ice creams were displayed.

"Come along, girls." Ms. Rapscott guided them through the crowd of people.

The clerks all had the same hairstyle that twirled around their heads three times and came to a perfect curl at the top, like frozen custard on a cone. They wore the same white jackets and pants with sparkly fur trim, and not one of them was any taller than Ms. Rapscott's girls.

The store was a beehive of activity, and there was a sense of urgency, as if it were Christmas Eve and people had only moments to buy their last gifts.

"Why is everyone leaving?" Fay asked.

It was true, customers streamed passed them. A woman with three little boys, licking triple-decker cones hurried by. "It's going to *storm*," she said to Ms. Rapscott in an irritated voice, with the emphasis on "storm," as if she thought it was very bad judgment on the teacher's part to be leading her class into the store instead of out of it, like she was.

"Don't pay any attention to *her*," Ms. Rapscott stuck her nose in the air. "And whatever you do, *don't* look for Dahlia Thistle."

In spite of what she was told, Fay searched the faces of the little kids being rushed along by their teacher, a thin man with large eyeglasses and a bow tie, who clapped his hands every few seconds and nervously called out orders. "Stay in line, class! No talking! Let's go! Let's go!" A straggler with chocolate ice cream still smeared around his mouth gave the girls a worried look. "It's going to—" but before he could finish his sentence the teacher grabbed his hand and yanked him away.

Moving against the current, the girls pushed through the throng to a counter with a chubby clerk who had a name tag just below her left shoulder that said: INGRID. Her cheeks were rosy from the cold and so plump that they pushed her blue eyes upward and made them look squinty.

Ding-Dong! Ding-Dong! Suddenly doorbell sounds chimed and a woman's voice came over the PA system. "Attention, Alps customers! We are now closed due to the inclement weather! Please exit toward the front of the store!" *Ding-Dong! Ding-Dong!*

"Hurry! Hurry!" Ingrid fluttered her chubby fingers at the girls.

Ms. Rapscott and the corgis quickly picked out three different flavors of ice cream. "We'll have a gallon each of moonlight white chocolate, peppermint watermelon, and lavender cream puff, please."

Ingrid filled the order with lightning speed, collected the money, handed the paper bag to one of the corgis, and said, "Good-bye! We're about to close!" She grabbed a towel and began to wipe off the top of the counter that the girls were standing in front of.

Fay cried, "Close? You can't! We're here to look—I mean *not* to look—for our classmate, Dahlia Thistle!"

"Precisely!" Mildred said, trying her best to sound like what she thought a Head Girl should.

"Absolutely!" Bea chimed in as well, hoping Ms. Rapscott had seen.

Ingrid's face was red with exertion. "Well, if you really don't want to find her, don't look in there." She pointed to a large stainless-steel door. Over it was the word: FREEZER.

"Thank you so much," Ms. Rapscott said politely. "That's exactly where we shall go to not look for her. Good day."

"You'd better hurry. It's going to storm," Ingrid said.

Annabelle hoped Ms. Rapscott wasn't looking, but she couldn't help herself. She placed the palms of her hands on the slanted glass barrier of the case and leaned forward until her face was inches from Ingrid the clerk. "Wait a minute—"

Annabelle said in her best I'm-going-to-get-to-the-bottom-of-this voice. "You're closing the store because it's going to storm?"

Ingrid just giggled, which made Annabelle even more determined. She narrowed her eyes, "That's ridiculous! It's seventy degrees and sunny outside."

Ingrid laughed almost uncontrollably, and her entire body jiggled. "Not outside—it's going to storm *inside*."

"Thrilling!" Ms. Rapscott exclaimed.

Annabelle's mouth dropped open as it did whenever she was surprised. "It can't storm *inside*!" Annabelle sputtered. "I've read the entire *Encyclopedia Britannica*—I know!"

But no sooner were the words out of her mouth than a snowflake drifted down and landed on Annabelle's nose. She gasped and touched it with both hands to make sure it wasn't just a speck of dust. Ingrid reached over and with a swipe of her towel wiped Annabelle's fingerprints off the glass where her hands had been, spun around, and scurried away.

In seconds the snow was coming down so hard they could barely see.

"Come along, girls." Ms. Rapscott opened the freezer door.

Mildred ran toward it, but as usual Bea, Fay, and Annabelle got there first. As soon as they were all through, the door slammed shut with a *BANG!*

Chapter 15

MT. EVERBEST ACADEMY FOR BOYS OF BUSY PARENTS

"Where are we?" Bea said.

Off in the distance there were mountains as far as the eye could see.

Fay was puzzled. "I thought we were supposed to be in a freezer."

"A freezer?" Ms. Rapscott peered through her binoculars. "Anyone can see this is not a freezer, Fay, though it *is* freezing. Mittens are in your pockets, girls!"

Sure enough they were standing on a road that zigzagged to the top of a mountain and the signpost said: LESS TRAVELED ROAD. Ms. Rapscott pointed out tiny footprints in the snow.

"Dahlia Thistle?" Fay said incredulously.

"When you stop looking, you find things where you least expect them." Ms. Rapscott repeated her Remark of the Day just as Lewis and Clark hurried off, their scarves fluttering out behind them. The clouds parted for a moment, and at the top of the mountain something glittered. "Follow the light, girls!" Ms. Rapscott called over her shoulder as she charged after the corgis up Less Traveled Road.

Bea, Fay, and Annabelle were excited as well, and even Mildred raced after her. Slate gray clouds hung heavy and low, hiding any trace of the sun, but the snow had stopped and they all kept a close eye on the footprints. Up, up, up they hiked as fast as they could.

Just before they reached Ms. Rapscott and the corgis near the top, Fay spotted something on the side of the road. It was a familiar looking blue wrapper with the words: "*Rapscott Cracking Good Crackers*" written across the top in white. Fay was excited that someone had been there before them—someone with Rapscott Crackers—and she knew that someone could only be one person. "Look!" Fay shouted, and quick as can be Bea plucked it out of the snow to show the teacher.

Ms. Rapscott studied the wrapper, then handed it to Clark, who carefully deposited it in a plastic bag and put it in his backpack. "A Rapscott Girl never litters, class—except when she becomes lost—then it is perfectly acceptable to leave a clue!"

The light on the summit winked clearer now. They all walked together up the steep slope with renewed energy. It was dark by the time there was no higher place to go, and they strained their eyes to see.

"There it is!" Fay shouted.

"I see it! I see it!" Bea cried.

"I see it, too!" Mildred said. Of course, following the light had not inspired Annabelle in the least, but her heart still skipped a beat when she saw this one. It was so similar to the one atop their own school.

THWACK! THWACK! THWACK! All at once they were being bombarded with snowballs.

They ducked to avoid being hit and then threw some back.

A deep voice bellowed, "Stop it! Stop it this minute!" The girls could see a large, white furry bear coming out of the darkness. "No! No!" he scolded the five little bears, and they dropped their ammunition. But as they got closer, Bea, Mildred, Fay, and Annabelle could see that the large creature wasn't a bear at all but a man wearing a furry white hat, jacket, and pants, and the snowball throwers weren't five little bears but five boys in the same kind of white furry outfit.

"What brings you all the way to the top of my mountain?" the man asked.

"We're not looking for a student of mine," Ms. Rapscott replied.

"Truly the only way to find something," the man agreed heartily.

"My thoughts exactly!" Ms. Rapscott declared. "I suppose you wouldn't happen to have not seen Dahlia Thistle?"

"Come and not see for yourselves!" The man heaved open a solid oak door to what looked like a cross between an enormous igloo and a miniature castle and disappeared inside. The boys stood looking at the girls nastily.

"Go away!" one boy yelled, and pulled Mildred's hair. She yelped, and they all snickered rudely.

"Dahlia Thistle fell off the mountain!" another boy said.

"I pushed her!" said another.

"Go away or you'll be sorry!" said a fourth boy.

The last made a horrible face at the girls before he and the rest scurried in through the door.

Ms. Rapscott strode after them and all the girls gasped. "Wait! Don't go!" Mildred called out, but to no avail, for Ms. Rapscott was a teacher who loved nothing better than a pack of rude, wild boys. The girls waited to see if the teacher would come back, and when she didn't Mildred stood outside covering her eyes while Bea, Fay, and Annabelle peeked inside.

It was a round room with stone walls. There were hundreds of books on shelves that went all the way up to the ceiling; a map of the mountain rolled down like a window shade; a clock on the wall that said 5:07; a chalkboard, paint boxes, crayons; one large desk in front of six little ones; and in the center of the boys, and the man, and Ms. Raspcott was a small girl.

She waved at the girls and said, "I'm Dahlia Thithle!"

"That's thi-s-s-s-stle, Dahlia," Ms. Rapscott said. "You must enun-ci-ate."

"Thithle," Dahlia said back.

"I have your lamb!" Fay ran to the girl. She proudly pulled the stuffed animal out of her pocket, and the look on Dahlia Thistle's face was every bit as excited and happy as Fay had imagined it would be.

Dahlia pressed her face into his fur, "Harold!" she murmured, and Fay could have sworn she heard the stuffed lamb sigh.

Ms. Rapscott's girls gathered around Dahlia Thistle. They were so happy to have finally found her—even Bea, who wouldn't be able to take credit for the rescue—that they would have hugged one another, except their parents were so busy they had never showed them how. Lewis checked his watch, and Clark wrote down 5:10, the exact time that the lost girl was found.

The man apologized to the girls for the boys' awful behavior and bowed deeply. "I am Mr. Everbest, Headmaster of Mount Everbest Academy for Boys of Busy Parents."

"What a coincidence!" Ms. Rapscott smiled broadly. "I am *headmistress* of Great Rapscott School for *Girls* of Busy Parents!" Lewis and Clark nodded.

"Astounding!" he cried, and ladled cups of hot chocolate that steamed in the hearth for everyone. Bea, Mildred, Fay, and Annabelle warmed their hands on their mugs, taking small sips as it cooled, while Ms. Rapscott and the corgis observed the five boys with curiosity. They sat in a line on a long bench next to the fire with sour expressions on their faces.

"What's your name?" Ms. Rapscott said cheerfully to a short chubby boy.

"Theodore," he replied glumly, and stuck out his tongue and crossed his eyes.

"Theodore is Known for Making Horrible Faces," Mr. Everbest explained.

Ms. Rapscott clapped her hands. "But you know, Mr. Everbest, that is a sure sign of an extraordinarily gifted artist."

"Yes, and he has large earlobes, and those sorts always have a good sense of humor." Mr. Everbest then went on to introduce the other boys, and the girls learned that Oscar, who was thin and pale, was Known for Being Sickly, but he had thick blond hair like a Viking and was a natural-born explorer. Nathan had a lazy eye and was Known for Running Around in Circles Until He Fell Down, but he had an extraordinary lifeline on the palm of his hand and would most likely live to two hundred and thirty-five. Ernest was the tallest and Known for Making Rude Noises, but there was far more to him than that because he also had a cowlick on the crown of his head, which was a sure indication he had nerves of steel. Reggie was Known for Holding His Breath Till He Turned Purple, but he had a sympathetic nature and would be a tireless defender of the downtrodden someday. One was as different from the other, but each looked more miserable than the next.

"What's wrong with you?" Bea asked Theodore, and he pulled down his lower eyelids with two fingers of one hand and pushed up his nose with one finger of the other hand.

"UGH!" Bea turned away.

"He's just mad because you're going to take her with you," Reggie grumbled.

"Of course we are," Annabelle huffed. She had little patience with these immature boys.

"But I don't want her to go!" Reggie screamed, and started to hold his breath.

"Neither do I," Oscar moaned, and started to scratch because he got hives whenever he was upset.

"Me either!" Nathan began to twirl in circles, faster and faster, with his arms out like propellers.

"I don't either." Theodore squinched up his eyes and smooshed his face together with two hands.

"She's our friend!" Reggie said as he began to turn purple. "And we found her first!" Oscar itched, Nathan spun ever faster, and Ernest began to make disgusting slobbering sounds.

Dahlia stood up. "All of you stop it this instant!" She stamped her foot and pounded her little fists against her skinny thighs. "Listen to me." The boys stopped and gazed at her with wide serious eyes. "I *have* to go to my own school, but I can come back to visit." She kissed her lamb and placed him in the middle of the bench between the boys. "But while I'm gone I want you all to look after Harold for me. I'm afraid I might be too busy at Great Rapscott School."

"You didn't lisp," Theodore said incredulously. "Not even once!" The boys were all surprised, and Bea could have sworn that Dahlia Thistle had just grown about two inches.

"Congratulations, Dahlia, my girl!" Ms. Rapscott exclaimed. "You have just bloomed!"

"I have?" she said, for she really didn't feel any different at all.

"Yes, you have," Mr. Everbest nodded. "You may be a Late Bloomer, but You Are Wise Beyond Your Years."

"Precisely!" Ms. Rapscott said. Lewis checked on the time, and Clark wrote down 5:25 so that they would always know exactly when Dahlia Thistle bloomed.

"But can't she stay?" Reggie asked, and the rest of the boys joined in pleading pitifully. And now the girls understood that the boys weren't really a pack of horrible scoundrels, they just appeared that way, which is how it always is when you first meet Sons of Busy Parents.

"Could I?" Dahlia said, for even though she was a girl she really liked it at Mount Everbest School for Boys. She had her own room and was learning tons of things that her parents had never had time to teach her. She didn't even mind wearing the boys' school uniform.

Ms. Rapscott closed her eyes and breathed in deeply like she did whenever she had an important decision to make. "Well . . . summer session is about over . . . and I suppose it wouldn't hurt for her to stay on here until the fall." Everyone looked expectantly and finally Ms. Rapscott said, "Yes."

"YAY!" All the boys shouted and looked happy for the first time.

"It's settled then," Ms. Rapscott said. "I will send her box along promptly, Mr. Everbest. She's only to be mailed home if she passes all the required tests to your satisfaction. Regardless, please make sure she is at Great Rapscott School by the beginning of the fall semester, September tenth."

He agreed and good-byes were said all around. When Ms. Rapscott and her girls stepped out into the night and walked around to the back of the school, far below and off in the distance blinked the Great Rapscott lighthouse.

"Good-bye, Dahlia!" Ms. Rapscott's girls shouted.

"See you in September!" Dahlia shouted back.

Ms. Rapscott called to Mr. Everbest, "And whatever you do, don't forget to pull off the kwik-close tape to secure the E-Z shut flaps before you send her!"

Chapter 16

TO THE END OF LESS TRAVELED ROAD

Bea, Mildred, Fay, and Annabelle were soon on their way to the end of Less Traveled Road. Ms. Rapscott and Lewis and Clark had gone ahead and were nowhere in sight, but the girls weren't afraid. The lighthouse burned brightly and now all of them—especially Mildred—felt a surge of enthusiasm to get there quickly.

The air was damp and raw with large thunderclouds marching in from the west. "It can't be far now," Bea muttered. A sign along the side of the road said: DEAD END. "The lighthouse must be right around that corner."

They jogged now. The beam of light from Great Rapscott School for Girls of Busy Parents seemed to fill the sky. Up ahead, silhouetted in the lamplight, Ms. Rapscott and Lewis and Clark waved them on. They raced down the sandy road with the beach grass growing down the middle of it.

"Hurry! Hurry!" the teacher called.

As tired as they were from the day's adventure, the girls sprinted toward the finish, backpacks bouncing, snow boots pounding. They pumped their arms for speed. Bea was out in front, carried by her sturdy little legs, with Fay, and then Annabelle behind her. Mildred was still the slowest, and she gulped for air with every stride. She didn't want the teacher to see her last—*again*.

All the while the Great Rapscott beacon revolved around and around, shining through the dark to light their way.

"Almost there!" Ms. Rapscott called out.

Bea exploded through the door. She was first and hoped Ms. Rapscott had noticed.

Fay skidded in behind her.

Annabelle slid across the classroom floor and slammed into Bea and Fay.

With a burst of speed that Mildred never even knew she possessed, she hurtled over the threshold and landed in a heap under the clock.

All four girls lay sprawled on the floor, gasping for breath in various states of relief, well-being, and exhaustion. Lewis and Clark had run off to place the three gallons of ice cream in the freezer, while Ms. Rapscott was already out of her down clothing and back in her familiar oversized fishermen's sweater, mud brown pants, and boots. She stood before them with her hands clasped and beamed at the girls. "Because you have all behaved today as true Rapscott Girls, I have a surprise."

The girls glanced nervously at one another, for they weren't sure they liked the idea of a surprise from Ms. Rapscott. "What now?" Mildred groaned quietly to herself. But there was no saying "no" to Ms. Rapscott.

"Come along, girls," the teacher ran up the spiral stairs, and the girls followed, wondering what would happen next. Past the kitchen, the bathroom, their dorm, and they continued to climb up into Ms. Rapscott's room that looked like the inside of a ship's cabin with the bed like a boat. She turned on the stairs, and her eyes sparkled the way they did just before anything strange was about to happen. Then she disappeared to the next forbidden floor.

One by one the girls climbed the spiral stairs, and as soon as their heads popped through the hatch to the sixth floor, they were so surprised they were speechless, except for Bea who whispered, "Pajamas?"

"Every sort ever made in the entire world!" Ms. Rapscott said confidently. "I'm sure you'll find exactly what you want."

"Do you have pink pajamas with ducks on them?" Mildred asked.

Ms. Rapscott rushed over to a rack of pink pajamas and started going through them. *Clink! Clink! Clink!* went the hangers as she pushed one after the other with expert speed. "Pink pajamas with hearts, stripes, penguins, stars, poodles, snowmen, candy canes, ponies . . . how about ponies?" She held them up for Mildred to see.

Mildred shook her head.

"Pink pajamas with plaid . . . roses . . . clouds . . ." Ms. Rapscott muttered to herself. "I know they're *here*! Bunnies . . . cats . . . DUCKS! Pink pajamas with ducks—there you go!" she said triumphantly.

Mildred rubbed them up against her cheek. "Mmmmm, soft."

The teacher instructed the girls to each pick out three pairs of pajamas.

Bea started going through several of the warm flannel kind, and she found one pair of blue with white snowflakes and two pairs of white with blue snowflakes because she wanted to always remember the Alps.

Mildred had her pair of pink pajamas with the ducks on them, plus one pair of pink pajamas with ponies, and one with candy canes.

Fay found three pretty purple nightgowns with ruffles on the front, collar, and sleeves, and a hem that would be completely impractical for mopping floors in.

Annabelle picked out the extremely practical nightshirts with pinstripes and polka dots in green because that was her favorite color now.

Of course, Ms. Rapscott and Lewis and Clark already had their durable fleece pajamas that would keep them warm there in the Big White Lighthouse by the Sea where they loved how the weather was always bad.

Bea wondered aloud to Ms. Rapscott, "There must be 100,823 pairs."

"There are 100,999, to be exact," Ms. Rapscott said.

"Where did you get all these pajamas?" Bea wanted to know.

Ms. Rapscott replied with a faraway look in her eyes, "Many years ago, I found myself on Less Traveled Road, and when I got to the end, I said to myself, 'Wouldn't it be nice right now to have a good pair of pajamas!' Then I thought anyone who makes it all this way has really accomplished something. And maybe they deserve to see a friendly face and have someone be here to give them a pat on the back. And maybe, even if they didn't find what they were looking for, at least they'd have the finest pair of pajamas guaranteed to give them the best night's sleep and the sweetest dreams forever and ever." Ms. Rapscott dipped in her pocket and pulled out the wishbone. "And that is when I made my third wish."

"You wished for a roomful of pajamas!" The girls laughed.

"And here they are." Ms. Rapscott smiled.

Bea, Mildred, Fay, and Annabelle took their pajamas with them down the circular stairway, and after they had their tea and pie and moonlight white chocolate ice cream from the Alps, they washed their faces, brushed their teeth, and changed into their new pajamas. They were eager to see if Ms. Rapscott had been right.

That night thunder cracked, and jagged streaks of lightning blazed across the sky. The wind tore over the sea, and waves crashed in a cacophony that would have unnerved the ordinary child. But Ms. Rapscott's girls had grown to love the sound because they knew that no matter how bad the weather was, they were always safe inside the big white lighthouse.

Sure enough, snug in their new pajamas, the girls fell into a deep slumber as soon as they put their heads on their pillows, where they had the sweetest dreams ever.

Chapter 17

THE RAPSCOTTIAN MEDAL

The next morning Ms. Rapscott looked very pleased as she waited with Lewis and Clark underneath the ticking clock on the wall. There was no drawing of the birthday cake on the chalkboard, as they had come to expect at the end of each week. Instead, Lewis wore an officious expression, and the way he held a mysterious-looking briefcase with a large brass lock—flat like a tray, as if it contained the crown jewels—made the girls squirm in their seats and titter with anticipation.

"Ms. Rapscott!" Bea raised her hand. "Aren't we going to do the Top of the Birthday Cake today?" She had been looking forward to it all week since she was sure that she would be at the top again.

"I have something *even better* in store for you today." Ms. Rapscott's eyes glittered. The girls exchanged worried glances and muttered to one another about what the teacher was up to now.

She put a finger to her lips for quiet and said, "Now, class, how do you know when you have *officially* found your way?"

Annabelle definitely knew the answer and for once she was right, "That's easy, you have officially found your way when you know exactly where you are!"

"Very good, Annabelle." Ms. Rapscott looked at her students one at a time. "Beatrice. Mildred. Fay. Annabelle. Do you know exactly where you are?"

"Great Rapscott School for Girls of Busy Parents!" they shouted.

"Congratulations, class! You have all demonstrated pluck, enthusiasm, spirit of adventure, brilliance, and self-reliance." Ms. Rapscott hopped once for joy. "You have officially passed the course How to Find Your Way!"

"YAY!" the girls cheered.

Clark ceremoniously opened Lewis's briefcase to reveal five medals. Each one was an eight-pointed bronze star with north, south, east, and west, on the corresponding points like a compass. The picture of a lighthouse was etched in the center with the words, RAPSCOTTIAN MEDAL, and around its edge was written, FOR FINDING YOUR WAY.

"You will wear these proudly on your uniforms always," Ms. Rapscott said earnestly. The medal was attached to a blue and silver ribbon. Lewis and Clark shook each girl's hand as Ms. Rapscott pinned the awards on their uniforms. She took the last medal and held it high to face the window. "Congratulations, Dahlia Thistle!" Then she placed it in her desk drawer for safe keeping until the girl's arrival for the fall semester.

When she was done the teacher stood before the girls and looked deeply into their eyes to make absolutely sure they understood. "You will not go back the way you came, you will always take Less Traveled Road, you will look for the light, and then you will forever know how to find your way."

The girls nodded and looked back at her in a way that made her sure they had learned their lessons well. Then there was laughter, and talk, and ice cream, and birthday cake, and Bea, Mildred, Fay, and Annabelle admired their medals, which made them feel brave just to wear.

The girls were so excited from the morning's festivities that they were completely caught off guard at the end of lunch when Ms. Rapscott made an unexpected announcement. "Today, class, you will be going home!" The chatter instantly stopped. "Your boxes will be ready for departure at exactly one p.m." She dabbed her lips with her napkin and ushered the girls down to the classroom.

Suddenly they had lost all their exuberance.

Their smiles were gone, and their shoulders sagged.

"But I don't want to go!" Bea sat down hard on her desk chair. "There's nothing to do there except count cinder blocks!"

"And watch TV," Mildred cried.

"And mop the floors!" Fay moaned.

"And read the encyclopedia." Annabelle stamped her foot.

In spite of their pleas, Lewis checked his watch, and Clark continued to put the last few things in their backpacks.

The clock struck 1:00.

"Come along, girls!" Ms. Rapscott sailed out the door to the walkway with her charges trotting behind in single file, asking all kinds of questions.

Bea tugged at her fisherman's sweater. "But there won't be any ice cream and birthday cake at home!"

"Oh, please, can't I stay?" Mildred called breathlessly. "Who will be there to catch me if slip down a well?"

"Or if I plummet off a balcony?" Fay cried.

"Or if I get dragged out to sea!" Annabelle shouted.

"But Ms. *Rap*scott!" They were, by now, all in tears.

Outside, the four empty boxes waited.

"Remember, girls!" Ms. Rapscott gathered her students. "In addition to everything you have learned the last three weeks here at Great Rapscott School, please exercise caution with bees, bears, banana peels, oncoming cars, dump trucks, large holes, moldy bread, folding chairs, hot stoves, icy roads, and falling trees, and you will all remain safe and sound!"

"But ho-o-o-o-o-w?!" Annabelle wailed. "Our parents don't care for us a smidge!"

"It's not that your parents don't care for you; it's just that they're *busy*, Annabelle," Ms. Rapscott explained. Bea, Mildred, Fay, and especially Annabelle all thought her a heartless teacher to send them back to such parents.

Lewis and Clark seemed unmoved as well and set to hoisting the girls into their boxes. Bea,

Mildred, and Fay were moistly saying good-bye to one another, certain that they would never survive until the next semester. Annabelle kept repeating, "Ms. Rapscott! Ms. Rapscott!" trying to get her teacher's attention to ask a question, but Ms. Rapscott was saying, "Hurry! It's time!"

The ocean was noisy with waves, and the seagulls screamed and swooped through the air.

When the girls were finally all in their boxes, Ms. Rapscott stood before them with her hands clasped together. "There are many more tests ahead, girls, and it's not going to be easy!" She made a little hop for joy, and her eyes were laughing. "The fall semester begins on September tenth. Be aware that your boxes will be ready to transport you back to school promptly at six a.m. that morning."

There was only time for Bea to yell, "Good-bye, Mildred! Good-bye, Fay!" She hesitated for a second as her eyes met Annabelle's.

Annabelle flashed a lopsided grin and said timidly, "I'm sorry that I said you stink, Bea."

"I'm sorry that I short sheeted your bed and put cold noodles in your shoes," Bea said back, and Annabelle waved good-bye. "Good-bye, Annabelle!" Bea called just before Lewis peeled off the kwik-close tape on the E-Z shut flaps to seal the box. Bea already felt lonely, but a little reading light clicked on, and when she looked inside her backpack there was her notebook where she'd written down all the things that Ms. Rapscott had taught them over the last three weeks. She began to read: *PLUCK: courageous readiness to fight or continue against all odds.*

"Wow," Bea whispered. "That's me." She flipped through the pages past all the lessons: How to Make Hot Chocolate, How to Ride a Bike, What to Do for a Stomachache, The Proper Way to Use a Q-tip. Bea settled into the soft packing material and reached for her crackers and cheese, because she always liked to eat when she read.

As soon as Mildred's box was shut, her reading light clicked on, too. Mildred sniffed a few times. She should be learning a lesson right now—like How to Waltz or How to Clip Your Toenails—

not sitting in a box on her way home where all there was to do was watch TV. She pulled out her notebook and pen and began to write: Hello, My name is Mildred A'Lamode, and I am a student at Ms. Rapscott's School . . . she stopped for a second to dry her eyes and continued: My parents were busy so I got sent here. I used to watch TV all the time and was afraid to leave my room and then one day . . .

Inside her box, Fay thought about mops and stared dejectedly at her feet. Her socks had fallen in a crumpled heap around her ankles again, but she couldn't help but smile as she reached down to pull them up. They would all be together again soon—even Dahlia Thistle. And Fay began to think about the adventures they might have next semester at Great Rapscott School, which is how it is when you have a Sparkle in Your Eye.

"Wait a minute!" Annabelle held up her hand with her palm out in a stop sign just as Clark was about to seal the E-Z shut flaps. "Is this box going to fly?"

245

"Fly?" Ms. Rapscott said indignantly. "Whoever heard of boxes that fly?"

Annabelle narrowed her eyes and stared at the teacher for a long time, and Ms. Rapscott stared back until Annabelle soon started to think it silly and preposterous (even for Ms. Rapscott) to think that the boxes could actually fly. "Oh, what will become of us?" Annabelle sighed as she lowered herself into the box.

"You are Rapscott Girls, Annabelle." Ms. Rapscott waved for Clark to close the box. "The sky's the limit!"

A sheet of navy blue clouds was coming in off the ocean. High above, the school flag began to snap against the pole, and the sign creaked as it blew back and forth on its hinges. A huge gust of wind, as fierce as a freight train barreling down the tracks, suddenly whooshed in off the ocean. Whether it was the wind or the boxes themselves was impossible to say, but all four lifted off the ground, nosed their way upward, and circled around the lighthouse.

"Thrilling!" Ms. Rapscott muttered.

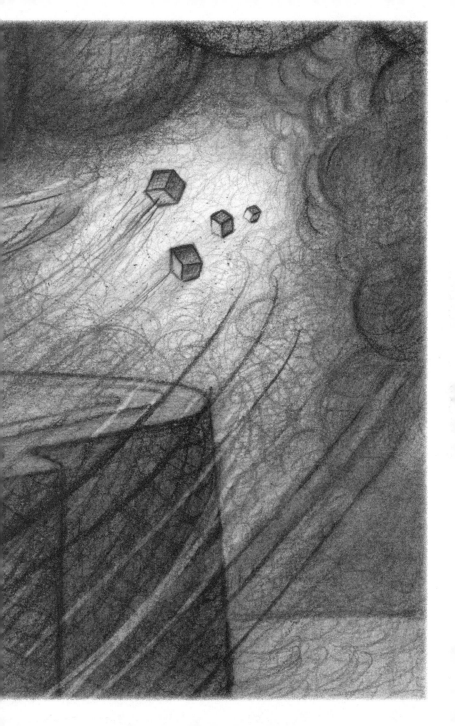

There was a loud clap of thunder. Another storm was coming.

The beacon rotated above them, slowly shining its light out into the busy world for all to see. "There they go, boys." Ms. Rapscott blew her nose and Lewis's and Clark's tails drooped. "But they'll be back for next semester and it'll be just in time for hurricane season." The corgis grinned, and Ms. Rapscott shouted over the crashing waves, "I can hardly wait!"

She peered through her binoculars as Bea, Mildred, Fay, and Annabelle disappeared over the horizon.

ACKNOWLEDGMENTS

Ms. Rapscott's favorite heroine Amelia Earhart once said, "Adventure is worthwhile in itself!" and creating *Ms. Rapscott's Girls* has indeed been an adventure that I've shared with many.

First and foremost I would like to thank my brilliant editor, Nancy Conescu, Known for Being Wildly Creative, whose enthusiasm for the book and encouragement over the last three years, not to mention her love of Dance Moms, were indispensable in the making of *Ms. Rapscott's Girls*.

Next a big thanks to Jenny Kelly, art director extraordinaire and a true Rapscott Girl in every sense of the word. Known for Working Tirelessly to Make Things Right, Jenny belongs on top of the birthday cake.

Ditto Lily Malcom who, like a good cantaloupe, is loaded with excellent taste and whose art direction and input were essential in the making of *Ms. Rapscott's Girls*.

Also I would like to extend my heartfelt thanks to the talented Judythe Sieck for her beautiful calligraphy on the cover. My Rapscott rain bonnet goes off to you!

Thanks as well to president and publisher of Dial Books for Young Readers, Lauri Hornik, a woman of substance who could rival Ms. Rapscott herself. Known for Sticking to Her Guns but also for Being a Straight Shooter who definitely has a sparkle in her eye.

This brings me to Kate Harrison, who is about to become Known for her Bravery and Courage as she steps forth into the great unknown. Kate always strives to be like a good pair of boots: sturdy, durable, and waterproof, which will serve her well as she sets out to accompany me on a new adventure to Great Rapscott School for Girls of Busy Parents.

Lastly I would like to thank the real Great Rapscott in jolly old England which remains my greatest adventure, where I drew my inspiration and where I first learned How to Find My Way lo so many years ago.